LEAVE IT TO ME

Born in Calcutta, Bharati Mukherjee now lives and
teaches in San Francisco. She is the author of seven
novels, most recently *The Holder of the World*.

BY BHARATI MUKHERJEE

The Holder of the World
The Tiger's Daughter
Wife
Darkness
The Middleman and Other Stories
Jasmine
Leave it to Me

WITH CLARK BLAISE

Days and Nights in Calcutta
The Sorrow and the Terror

Bharati Mukherjee

LEAVE IT TO ME

V

VINTAGE

Published by Vintage 1998

2 4 6 8 10 9 7 5 3 1

First published in Great Britain by
Chatto & Windus 1997

Vintage
Random House, 20 Vauxhall Bridge Road,
London SW1V 2SA

Random House Australia (Pty) Limited
20 Alfred Street, Milsons Point, Sydney
New South Wales 2061, Australia

Random House New Zealand Limited
18 Poland Road, Glenfield,
Auckland 10, New Zealand

Random House South Africa (Pty) Limited
Endulini, 5A Jubilee Road, Parktown 2193,
South Africa

Random House UK Limited Reg. No. 954009

A CIP catalogue record for this book
is available from the British Library

ISBN 0 09 941511 9

Printed and bound in Great Britain by
Mackays of Chatham PLC

For David Fechheimer,

unraveler of myth and mystery

Leave It to Me

Prologue

In Devigaon, a village a full day's bus ride into desert country west of Delhi, old Hari tells of times before the "long ago" of fairy tale, when celestials battled demons and the Cosmic Spirit revealed itself in surprising forms to devotees. The story that children beg him to repeat at twilight—that smoky quarter hour most full of menace—is of Devi, the eight-armed, flame-bright, lion-riding dispenser of Divine Justice. They know that the Cosmic Spirit (assuming the appearance of gods) continually makes, unmakes and remakes the world they live in. They know that it also created goddess Devi and endowed her with the will to save and the strength to kill, and that it charged her with the mission of slaying the Buffalo Demon who had usurped the throne in the kingdom of heavenly beings.

And in this village, named after the serene slaughterer of a demon king, the children already know the story's ending. Before twilight blackens, Devi will blow the conch-shell call, and brandish in her many arms a lasso, a trident, a fire-tipped spear, a demon-splitting disc, a bow and arrows, a death-dealing staff, a thunder-sparking axe, a pitcher of water and necklace of blessed beads, and will head her soldiers on lionback. The Buffalo Demon, inheritor of the brute strength and physical appearance of his buffalo mother and the deceit and rage of his demon father, cunning, and magical powers, will vanquish her men. Some of Devi's soldiers the Buffalo Demon will gore to death; others he will stomp, still more fell with the tempest blasts of his panting breath, and lacerate with the whip-crack of his tail. Then he'll let loose the full ferocity of his bestial hate on the Earth itself. With his hooves, the Buffalo Demon will scour canyon-deep trenches; with his horns, he will shred the sky and scoop out mounds of soil as high as mountains; with his tail, he will churn the calm waves of the ocean into fatal hurricanes. And just as he is about to declare himself destroyer of gods and goddesses, Devi will muster the full powers of vengeance. She will fling her lasso around the demon neck, pierce, strike and slash the demon flesh, pin that demon bulk to the ground with her foot and cut off the usurper's buffalo-head.

While the children, comforted by story, curl into sleep on their bed-pallets, the Cosmic Spirit will smile on its daughter-goddess, then go back to creating, preserving, breaking and re-creating the cosmos as always.

And Devi? The Earth Mother and Warrior Goddess wipes demon blood off weapons and puts them away for the next time they are needed.

Part One

Part One

I can almost touch the diamond-hard light of stars and the silky slipperiness of leaves, almost taste smoke softer than clouds and sweeter than memory, almost feel God's breath burn off my sins.

What have I done but what my mothers did? The one who gave me birth, and the one I am just beginning to claim. Like them, I took a god of a special time and place as my guide.

My mothers, luminous as dewdrops in dawnlight, weightless as the wings of a newborn dragonfly, float towards me from the place where I was born. I have no clear memory of my birthplace, only of the whiteness of its sun, the harshness of its hills, the raspy moan of its desert winds, the desperate suddenness of its twilight: these I see like the pattern of veins on the insides of my eyelids.

I tell myself I must have been left unattended in the sun. Maybe the sand-yellow sun was low in the morning sky and whichever Gray Sister was charged with caring for me had been detained in the fields as the sun mounted. I don't want to believe it was an overcrowded orphanage's scheme to rid itself of a bastard half American. One murder attempt is enough. Some days while shoveling snow off the stoop in Schenectady, I have smelled heady hibiscus-scented breezes; I have felt tropical heat and humidity.

Tonight, in the cabin of this houseboat off Sausalito as curtains of flame dance in the distance and a million flash-bulbs burn and fizzle, and I sit with the head of a lover on my lap, the ferrous taste of fear invades me as though my whole body were tongue.

For all official purposes, like social security cards and unemployment benefits, I am, or was, Debby DiMartino, a fun-loving twenty-three-year-old American girl. I was adopted into a decent Italian-American family in the Hudson Valley. That's the upside of adoption. And believe me, I've approached this situation, *my* situation, from every angle. The downside is knowing that the other two I owe my short life to were lousy people who'd considered me lousier still and who'd left me to be sniffed at by wild dogs, like a carcass in the mangy shade.

The upside and the downside of being recyclable trash don't quite balance. Debby DiMartino is a lie. Whoever my parents intended for me to be never existed. That un-claimable part of myself is what intrigues me, the part that came to life in a desert village and had the name Baby Clear Water Iris-Daughter until it was christened in a Catholic orphanage. That's the part I want to remember. But there's another part I try to keep secret, the part that sings to moons and dances with stars. With everything I've done, I've tried to find a balance. It's just that Debby Di-Martino has no weight, no substance. I had to toss her out.

Cherchez le garçon. There was a boy, back when I was a stubby little thirteen-year-old. He was a twenty-two-year-old graduate student at Syracuse. I had no way of knowing there'd be a growth spurt—I was adopted—I only had my sister Angie to go by, which meant I had nothing to look forward to but getting fat and a puberty that would be a settling down, and out, and not a shooting up.

Wyatt was a lanky, crinkly-blond longhair (he had the first male ponytail I'd ever seen) getting a master's in social work, and I was his project. He had that low, slow, soft voice that just cries out sex, sex, sex! and deep brown eyes that bathed you with attention without ever blinking. The voice, the eyes, they burned at a very low flame, they never flared, but they consumed me just the same. He also had my police file, and he had the power if he ever wanted to use it to fuck up my future, all of which made our relationship an exciting kind of power trip.

Celia Montoya and I used to hang out at the mall, and one day (actually, many days) the temptation got too much and we "liberated" a little candy, some tapes, some perfume and panties—no problem—then we pushed our luck at Radio Shack since nothing was cooler that year than a portable phone. I should have figured out Radio Shack of all places would have some kind of electronic alarm. And the total value of the loot was over a hundred dollars, which automatically sent us to court and gave us a police record, and some sort of correction.

Pappy had connections in court and with the police. Celia had connections, too, but all the wrong kind, and she was out of school and in a facility for girls two days after her appeal. I never saw her again. Me, I got Wyatt, and a chance to erase my record. The penalty was I would do some service, I would read some books and write something about them, I'd stay in school and improve my grades, and I'd talk my problems out in a circle of troubled girls, as we were called, led by Wyatt. I got to stay in school and no one knew about the Circle, or Wyatt.

Celia would never have made it, she would have laughed in his face, or she would have stared at the floor. A couple of other girls couldn't take it either and said Wyatt's voice drove them to drugs and housebreaking. Wyatt was the first to ask me about adoption, what I knew, what I remembered. He put a lot of stress on it, and I know it would have upset Pappy if he'd known that rehabilitation meant bringing up feelings I didn't know I had.

"I've been reading your file, Debby," Wyatt'd say, once we were out of the Circle. "How did the DiMartinos come to adopt you?"

I'd never asked, and they'd never told. Lawyers, they always said, but it had to have started with the Church, all those little pledge envelopes for missions in Asia that Mama still fills out. I knew only that they'd found me in an orphanage run by Gray Nuns.

"You're not even interested?"

"I always figured it was fate."

"Schenectady was fate?"

Wyatt took me out to the animal shelter. It was where he'd worked on weekends and high school summers. It was the place that had formed his philosophy of life. It was the only place where the Ultimates sat side by side. "Love and Death," he said. "Kindness and Killing." He thought he could be the catcher in the pound; everything depended on his keeping his orphans clean enough, making them just a little more appealing, giving them cutesy names like Barbra, walking them and running them in the park. My family always called the animal shelter the pound, and I thought of it, if I thought of it at all, as an alternate lodging between loving homes. You don't usually visualize the dog pound as the palace of love. No one ever told me they gassed puppies and kitties.

"Cuteness is all that counts," Wyatt said. "You have a bad day, you wake up with a dry nose, with dull eyes, you take a nap, you scratch your fleas—it's your life."

"What are you saying?"

"I'm saying you've got a chance, don't blow it. You might never have made it out of that orphanage. Someone must have seen something."

And what could they have seen in a baby girl whose unnamed mother identified herself as Clear Water Iris-Daughter, and whose father, also unnamed, was called Asian National in the adoption papers? The nuns weren't interested in my origins, they didn't care about filling in the gaps of my life; they were into good works. It was the mid-seventies and I was just a garbage sack thrown out on the hippie trail.

There's no passion in the world like that of a thirteen-year-old girl; she'll do anything for love, or what seems like love. She'll interpret anything as a little sign, she'll believe anything he says, she'll do anything to prove herself worthy of his notice. And then the time will come when she begins to feel her own power. I was only thirteen, but I was a knowing thirteen when I didn't want to hide it, and mellow-voiced Wyatt was the first man I showed it to.

Our little Circle meetings grew shorter and shorter, our trips in the country longer and longer. There were motels in the afternoon, flowery pastures, canoe trips. I could ruin him if I wanted, and he knew it. He shared his stash (which I knew he had), and before long he was praising my orphan's maturity, the integrity of shoplifting in a consumer society and of course saying that I was older than my age (at least three years for his sake, I hoped).

Wyatt signed off on my parole, then dropped out of grad school. I had been a bad influence on him, he said. He decided to go to California and work for the Sierra Club or become a nature photographer. Human emotions were too difficult. But he left me with the most important prediction of my life, something that got me through high school and college, and even helps today. I was just a small, dark thing, and he said, "You know, Debby, I can tell you're going to be tall and beautiful very soon, and someday you're going to be rich and powerful." He thought he had everything to do with it.

After Wyatt left, I convinced myself that I was lucky to be an orphan. From the families I'd been given, I'd scavenge the traits I needed and dump the rest. If a person is given *lives* to live instead of just one life (Mama's favorite soap), especially lives she hasn't even touched, she'll be far better off for it. Once in a junior high English class, on assignment, when the other girls were composing little rhymed Hallmark verses about love, I raged in rhyming couplets against whole peoples who brawled inside me. The poem shocked me. It throbbed with pains I had no right to feel. That was the first time I'd really cut loose.

Mr. Bullock said, "Debby, that's deep," and he forced me to read the poem out loud in class. And the kids said, "Jeezus, it could be, like, a song, Debby!" which was their highest compliment. Then Mr. Bullock asked, "Have you read Sylvia Plath, Debby?" and I said I didn't know any of the senior high girls, and he laughed. "Then you're a natural poetic talent, Debby," which sounded to me as thrilling as a new zit on the nose. He invited me to join an after-school geek club. I attended twice, but its members were weird and I could feel how easy it would be to weird out too.

Until that poem, I'd been Debby DiMartino, second daughter of Manfred and Serena DiMartino, hardworking, religious parents. In junior high, I'd looked enough like my sister Angie to pass for a real DiMartino, and I expected to ripen and coarsen early, like Mama and like Angie. But I didn't thicken like Angie did, and by my senior year, I was the tallest one in the family, including Pappy. I stayed thin, clear-skinned, dark-haired, amazed at the assertiveness of my body. The gym teacher encouraged me to think volleyball scholarships, and Angie nagged at me to try out mail-order-catalog modeling. My senior portrait was just the kind of thing that you find in *People* magazine at the Price Chopper, one of those bad-hair, ugly-duckling pictures of some high school cheerleader gone bad or murdered or of some eventually famous movie star.

My junior-year growth spurt ended a few months too early, leaving me a shade below five-nine. I was a tall girl in a small school, a beautiful girl in a plain family, an exotic girl in a very American town. I'd always had this throaty whisper of a voice, couldn't raise it above a satiny purr, in a family of choir singers and a town of chirpy sopranos. But I wasn't tall, beautiful or exotic enough to trust any of it, and so I made up my mind to find out if I was someone special or just another misfit. I didn't write another poem, but I began to understand about mugged identities. There was something to nature over nurture, and to the tyranny of genes. But you pay for all the knowledge you've gained. How could I explain to a Schenectady DiMartino that destiny's the bully you can't outpunch or outsmart? That the Gray Nuns, Mama, Pappy, Angie, Mr. Bullock, Wyatt, the junior high geeks and creeps I've blown off fit into the Big Picture? I need to believe in the bigger picture. Most orphans do.

Who are you when you don't have a birth certificate, only a poorly typed, creased affidavit sworn out by a nun who signs herself *Sister Madeleine, Gray Sisters of Charity?* And that name? No mother's name, no father's name, just *Baby Clear Water Iris-Daughter* meticulously copied out, taking up two full lines, when *Father* and *Mother* with long spaces after them are just ink flecks of nonexistence. What are you when you have nightmares and fantasies instead of dates and statistics? And, in place of memory, impressions of white-hot sky and burnt-black leaves? Nothing to keep you on the straight and narrow except star bursts of longing?

We thought Mr. Bullock was giving us a routine assignment, but what if a junior high English teacher with hair
in his ears is an agent of destiny? He'd made us read a
Robert Frost poem about a bird flying off a snow-dusted
bough. "The Muse," he'd encouraged us, "notices the
humblest object and the tritest movement and turns them
into the gold of passion and poesy."

Mr. Bullock said he wanted for us to write about something we knew, something we knew so well that we didn't
see it anymore. And so I wrote about the lacy, summertime
shadows of the squat oak that Grandpa DiMartino had
planted in the backyard to celebrate his escape from the
Bronx—so the family story goes—the day he got the deed
to the Schenectady house, and that set me thinking that
the grandpa who'd planted that oak and landscaped the
garden and put in the lily pond was Angie's grandpa and
not mine after all. That made me hear tiny gypsy moth
jaws on the tender skin of stalks, and that made me remember other leaf patterns against other horizons. I wrote
another about the dogs I'd seen at the pound, pretending
that I was alone and that I was a dog myself. Take me,
love me, shelter me, my barking said. I felt more deeply
than Debby'd ever dared let herself feel. Words ribboned
out of me. And when the assignment was done, I felt
cheated of places I couldn't draw and of parents I didn't
miss. I blamed the poem for robbing me of what I'd never
owned. It was as if a psychic with a 900 number had said
to me through the poem, You're just on loan to the Di-
Martinos. Treat them nice, pay your rent, but keep your
bags packed.

Back then, in Schenectady, I waited for the call. Not to be a model or a poet, which was to be not extraordinary enough. The call would be to something more special, to satisfy the monstrous cravings of other Debbys hiding inside. I didn't envy Angie as I helped her into the Greyhound bound for Manhattan and her modest transformation of a Hudson Valley accent, hair color, clothes, muscle tone and skin. I knew by then that there was a life beyond the state lines waiting for me to slip into. Star Quality just plays taller and thinner and younger than it really is; second bananas just look older and fatter than they really are. All I'd have to do was be beautiful, be available, and my other life, my *real* life, would find me.

The summer I fell for Frankie Fong I was telemarketing Elastonomics out of an abandoned shopping mall near Schenectady. The Elastonomics frontman ran my job interview from his room at a Ramada Inn. He was a fat boy in a tight yellow shirt with a HI, I'M TONY TUCCIANI name tag. I knew I had the job because the first thing Tony said to me was "Okay, you're a natural." The second thing he said was "Miss DiMartino, you have the voice of a sexy nun." I waited for the third thing. I could tell what a strain it was for him to call me Miss DiMartino instead of sweetheart or Debby. Because I don't have trouble being kind to myself, I translated Tony's compliment to mean my voice came on as warm but implacable. I was so innocent back then that I didn't guess that the scratchy voice that got me in trouble in church choirs was thick and low not with sexy promise, but with scar tissue.

Elastonomics, Tony Tucciani explained, was the newest product manufactured in Asia by Fong Home Products, a multinational fitness equipment company. "We're in the business of promoting all-round well-being" is how he put it. Tony, then, offered some of FHP's tested–in–Hong Kong tips on making the sales pitch. Like, turn the question "Expiration date?" into a command. Like, if a sucker doesn't bite in four frames, cut him off. After that he made his move. Bending forward, he said, "In other words, Debby, leave his dick flapping in the wind."

I asked for him to practice me a couple of times. I'd had the usual upstate after-school and summer jobs, waiting tables, ringing up cash registers in the mall, demonstrating everything from sorbet makers to electric drills, but selling invisible fitness equipment for a Chinese company was a first. Tony wasn't worried about taking a risk on me, because I had this great telephone voice, he said, gritty and seductive, like I was lying naked in bed smoking raw Camels and swilling gin. I was going to ask him if he praised all his interviewees like this when he explained, "The boss doesn't do scripts anymore. Improv's his new shtick." Niceties over, he said, "So when we going out, Debby?"

I saw what I saw: sweaty-frontman longing, motel, fifteen minutes, cute girl wants the job, give it a shot. I did need the job; he was right about that. I said, "Zip it up, fat boy!" and slammed down an imaginary phone. Then, sweetly, "How was that? Did I come on a little too strong? Too rude?"

We both knew to keep my triumph low-key. "No, no, just testing," he mumbled. "Just don't mention fat. Guys who call in think they're not getting laid because they're fat. When you work the midnight-till-six shift, you'll get all types." Then he launched into the list of sales videos that FHP and I were going to blast the American consumer with.

"I did okay?"

"You were good," the frontman assured me. "Very good."

So I became the sexy nun with the 800 number selling contrition by UPS. The telemarketing job made it possible for me to move out of the DiMartino split-level. I'd graduated from SUNY-Albany earlier that week. It was time. The sad, fat people punching out 800 numbers weren't the only ones looking for change.

The surprise for me was that my callers were romantics. They believed in me, not in salvation through Elastonomics. They begged, *If I call back, how do I know I'll get you?* I made them effortless promises. Just ask for me, Helena. Or depending on the mood of the day, Staci, Traci, Eva, Magda, Desiree. Some nights I tried out thirty personas. My lies paid off. Loverboys and couch potatoes parted with bucks. What did they expect from me? Phone sex passing itself off as self-improvement, a date once they got in shape? *Sounds good, Roger! You never know, do you, Dave? Expiration date?*

Debby DiMartino's body might have been stuck in a cubicle in a failed mall, where fifty other telemarketers for eight hours a night were talking up rock-'n'-roll CDs, scam cruises, fat-burner pills, discontinued cosmetics and underwear in XXL sizes, but I felt I'd broken free of Schenectady. Most of my callers assumed I was in Florida or in California. Sleepless in Jersey told me he smelled surf in my voice. *Three o'clock in the morning out here in East Orange, babe. Just midnight where you are, I bet.* I never let on I was deep into eastern time. The customer's always right. I'd never in my conscious life been out of eastern time, never west of Niagara Falls or south of Atlantic City. *Hawaii, actually!* the telephone voice taunted. *Sun's just going down. It's lei and luau time . . . Expiration date?*

Mixed in with the dreamers, I got my share of jerks. *Doesn't it get to you, taking calls at three in the morning from slobs like me?* The perverts had meaner questions. *I know you, girl. Men don't do it for you, do they?*

A marketing major, I didn't need the boss to tell me I was very good at pushing his exercise gizmo, but he did. On my last night shift in June. He phoned me at my cubicle from somewhere overseas where tonight was already tomorrow. A kittenish voice came on first. "Hello, this is Cynthia, Mr. Francis's personal assistant . . ." I stopped the voice right there. "I don't accept an order that isn't called in by the client himself or herself." I heard a choking noise, then a click, a couple of smothered snorts or laughs and finally "Mr. Francis does not dial calls himself. He is a very busy man." This time, Cynthia's words had a speakerphone echo to them. Kids at a slumber party having fun at my expense. "Then he should have known not to waste the time of a busy career woman," I snapped. "We aren't your give-us-your-credit-card-number-and-we'll-ship-you-hard-body-equipment kind of sleazy phone-order operation. If your Mr. Francis can't get off his butt to place the order himself, he can't be motivated to lose weight, shape up, turn his life around. You don't think that we sell Elastonomics to any and every plastic-dropping Joe Schmo, do you? Mr. Francis has to prove to us he's the kind of client Elastonomics wants. Get that message across. Then have him call us."

I didn't hang up. It was a slow night, which meant that a telephone tussle with Cynthia & Her Slumberettes was better than no call at all.

"Jolly good, Miss DiMartini!" A man's voice came over the phone. A man with a silky, Britishy accent was on the other end of the line, and not a prepubescent partybeast lowering her voice into a manly growl. "Splendid performance!"

"What did you just call me?"

"Anthony Tucciani was correct about you. You have a future with FHP."

"You know Tony Tucciani? You work for Tony? Is he monitoring us employees? Listening in without my permission, that has to be a felony."

"Tony? That's interesting. What if I said Mr. Tucciani is my employee?"

"Who are you, anyway?"

"What if I said I was Francis A. Fong, founder and CEO of Elastonomics? How would you address me?"

"Frankie!" I retorted. "But seriously, who told you . . ."

The man emitted long, tinkly laughter into the mouthpiece. Then he said, "For an American you have class, Miss DiMartini."

"DiMartino," I corrected. "Ends with an *o*, not with an *i* like Tony's."

"I'll be in touch. I'm calling from Kuala Lumpur, but Cynthia'll let you know when, Debby. I may call you Debby, mayn't I?"

The boss hung up without waiting for a yes or no from me. Given his *Masterpiece Theatre* voice and vocabulary,

I pictured Mr. Francis A. Fong as Bruce Lee playing Hugh Grant.

I didn't have to wait more than a week to meet him, and when I did, at the Indigo Club, the newest jazz place on Caroline Street in Saratoga Springs, the Chinese part of Frankie wasn't the first thing I noticed.

Okay, I have to call time out for a confession. Frankie Fong took me to dinner and to bed on the first date. And handed me keys to my first apartment three nights later. It was mesmerism at first sight. Not love; love's the surrender to guys you grew up with, and Frankie wasn't like anyone upstate. Let's say he leveraged me into dependence. You took in the hair, which was blue-black and wavy. You stared. The man had cheekbones, shoulders till Tuesday, a ballerina waist, bulging little buns: all of this you registered in a flash. Then you caught yourself staring, because he was smiling at you.

Frankie hadn't always been in the fitness equipment business. In his last incarnation, he'd been Francis "the Flash" Fong, star/director/producer of dozens of Hong Kong kick-boxing extravaganzas.

He was born Francis Albert Fong, named for you-know-who, in Hong Kong or maybe in Manila or Surabaya (catching him in a consistency meant he'd fallen in love with one of his wilder inventions), to Aloysius and Baby Fong. Every time he told his life story, he gave himself the luxury of a different hometown. I loved his made-up childhoods. His father, Aloysius Fong, with the freakishly Sinatra-like voice, was the Don Ho of a dozen South Asian Chinatowns. Baby, his mom, was Al's fourth wife. He'd lifted her from the chorus line of a Chinese opera in Manila. With Frankie, I traveled crazy worlds without ever leaving Saratoga.

" 'One for My Baby'—Dad *owned* that song in Asia. You ask any Chinese over seventy who wrote that song, who sang it, and they'll say it's Al Fong. They'll say Sinatra ripped Al off. 'One for my baby . . . One more for the road' . . . that's the way we lived. That's how we Chinese lived. Dad made it into a song of lost identity. That's why Sinatra sounds such a *whinge*, to tell the truth."

I studied the color photo of the crooner with pomaded hair and a gold-capped smirk. Frankie would never wear Al's blue satin jacket with the black velvet piping nor the gold lamé vest, but I could picture him—at twenty-two, at thirty-two—lounge-lizarding in a tacky Asian nightclub, cigarette in one hand, mike pressed to his lips with the other, eyes sparkling from the stage lights, the drops and the drugs, diamond cuff links glittering, karaokeing "My Way" to black marketeers and their mistresses. Those were Frankie's origins, before he stripped off the finery, slapped on a headband, became Flash and took to beating sense into outer-space aliens, cowboys, bikers, Maoists and French colonials in a series of kick-boxing spectaculars.

He didn't ask me about my origins, and I volunteered nothing. I was the innocent upstate Italian, playing a cameo role in my own life.

Frankie's memories of growing up on permanent tours of China-in-exile made squalor and malice sound educational. From the way he talked about life-from-a-suitcase in hotel rooms, I understood why owning showy property on Union Avenue was so important to him. I coveted property too, but a different kind of property. I coveted the deed to my shadowy parentage. To a cornered rat, hunger and greed, ambition and wish fulfillment, are synonyms.

Frankie needed to remember, and I needed to discover. He talked. But I wanted more; I wanted details, wanted to know the smell of fishing boats on Thai canals and the sound of monsoon rains on tin roofs. He reminisced. Of pariah dogs and flying foxes, floating bodies, ancient ruins, temple bells, Muslim calls, diesel fumes, painted "lorries." More hash than butter, he boasted. Fevers, drugs, backroom-behind-the-beaded-curtain Asia. Playing card games with child prostitutes between clients, singing for the madams, picking the pockets of American marines on R and R, chasing monkeys in grassy ruins, shimmying up slippery trunks of giant palms, packing his father's opium into false-bottomed trunks: Frankie made an Asian childhood sound great fun, something I wanted to claim, something I'd been robbed of. But by whom? By the California hippie who'd fucked a Eurasian thug so I could be born in that place, over there, where nightmare and poem merge? By the Gray Nuns who placed me oceans away from my orphan origins? By Pappy and Mama who believe love wipes misery clean?

From that night on I envied Frankie. As a boy he'd been everywhere the Chinese had settled: Calcutta, Bangkok, Saigon, Singapore, Manila, Jakarta, Sydney. He'd seen it all, the tin shacks and smoky dives of overseas Chinatowns, before assimilation or persecution closed them down. In Frankie's Asia, the streets were always hot, loud, smoky, full of cheats and drugs and whores; the night-clubs were always places of viciousness and degradation and carnality. From Frankie the Son's stories, I pictured Al the Dad, the sleek, hatchet-faced man with slicked-back, dyed hair, sitting offstage on a stool, alternately vomiting into a bucket and spraying his throat with a minty concoction mixed by Baby, then smoking a last cigarette down to Sinatra's approved length before making his entrance. Pappy became my dad a million times removed. Thanks to those stories, for the first time I felt connected. The DiMartinos were the aliens.

How could I explain all that to Frankie, who confided, "That's why I took up karate, you see. It was either that, or become Al Fong's little Michael Jackson."

He lingered on the books he'd devoured in libraries of faded hotels with colonial names, the Imperial, the Nelson Arms, the Lord Curzon. Had these same hotels been my backpacking mom's haunts? He'd self-educated himself, he confessed, on Dorothy Sayers and H. E. Bates, on leatherbound sets of Dickens, Bennett and Galsworthy. I'd never heard of any of these authors except Dickens, but I could feel my fingertips touching Moroccan-leather spines, could see the sparkle of gold dust rubbing off in my hands.

Forget the Asia that Mama raised mission money for, playing bingo every second Thursday night. From that night on, Frankie's stories of Asia replaced the video as foreplay. And my mystery father became a back-alley customer of almond-eyed whores, a hanger-on in all those clubs in all those cities that Aloysius Fong'd played.

"More!" I cried.

"What? There isn't any more."

"I want to know everything!"

"You're an exigent little tramp, aren't you?" But he said that after he blew me a kiss. Then he launched into a word game he made up for me.

"*First het sex with hermaphrodites in Hyderabad.*"

"*Jealous jockey jilted in Joliet . . .*"

"Ah, perfect, *my pleasing paramour, Deborah!* How about . . . *parked with prostitutes playing Parcheesi while his parents performed.* Your turn again, my dear."

"*Moi?* Let's see . . . *sultry, suburban, Schenectady school-girls studying suspicious signs of . . .*"

"Of what? *Of mystic mendicants meditating on meek-ness?*"

"No, *meditating on misted-over moons and menacing mango trees and missing mothers!*"

But it was just a game of words. It didn't express what I really felt about mothers discarding daughters. But Frankie's make-believe Asia of dogs and bats, heat, beggars, police sweeps, corruption, squalor, disease, transvestites, prostitutes, crows wheeling low over flat roofs, bony stray cattle ambling down muddy sidewalks, did stir up my desire for what might have been—must have been—a careless hippie mom's Asia. You see, this is one more side effect of adoption. I can imagine myself into any life; I can wrench myself away from a thousand backgrounds. I can assess damage, then just walk away. Nothing shocked me in Frankie's tales, nothing seemed absurd or false.

Frankie wasn't an immigrant the way that Paolo Di-Martino had been. No steerage, no crippling gratitude. Ask not what you et cetera; ask what your new country can do for you. Frankie intended to hang on to the fortune he'd made, and not let the mainland or any fool socialist system steal it from him. With Hong Kong about to go down the tubes, he said he'd decided to shift his assets, rebuild an empire and relocate his vast family somewhere within it. Five nations courted the Fongs' pool of liquid assets. Passports were offered in exchange for new investments. He'd done his homework; he'd scouted London, Vancouver and Toronto, Wellington and Auckland, Sydney and Perth, and chosen cheap and serene New York City.

Why not California, I asked. He favored me with his silky, superior smile. "I might never have met you in Ell-Lay." Which meant, too many Chinese in California. I might never have noticed him.

He put the complications of the Fong diaspora simply. "I signed; I paid; we filtered south and west," he said. The "we" included his aging parents, loutish uncles, layabout cousins, and fat-boy hangers-on, most of whom he employed in Fong Home Products or its parent company, Fong Family Growth Fund.

When he handed me the key to my apartment, he joked, "Now you, too, are part of the Fong Family Resettlement Scheme."

I took the key without argument. Angie, my sister, is still stuck in a one-bedroom four-share in the West Village, and Angie's twenty-seven. I don't keep up with the day-to-day politics of Albany let alone of Hong Kong, but

I was sure glad that China had timed its takeover for just the moment I came fully into *ripeness*. I was ready that July. Frankie didn't have a chance.

The apartment he rented for me was less than a mile from his own ten-bedroom Victorian on Union Avenue, with five baths and a wraparound porch wide enough for a jogging track. I never saw the inside. Frankie set some rules, the main rule being that he came to me, like some kind of old-time Chinese landlord. He was a new element in a traditional town, he apologized, he needed to come on as a respectable businessman. A cornered rat, I translated.

I liked this arrangement. I preferred he spend the nights in my place, among the clutter of vintage straw hats on dresser tops, the chintz dust ruffle I'd tacked together for the brass bed and the sepia-tinted family photos in oval frames. The family photos weren't of the DiMartinos nor of the Giancarellis, which was Mama's maiden name. I bought them in flea markets and at garage sales. Grim old grannies and stern grandpas in round collars and derby hats stared down at me making love to a Chinese immigrant and set their mouths just a little tighter.

Frankie wasn't a man of set habits. He was spontaneous in a scripted sort of way, the way good actors are. It must have been the Flash in him. Night after night he could deliver the same love grunts and bites, make the same smooth moves, and have them come across to me as unique, urgent, sincere. Back then, because I was into Improv in a big way, I didn't think to ask who scripted *my* part in the Fong-produced *Flash Kicks American Ass* extravaganza.

He brought over old Flash videos and walked me through each shot, tried to educate me about the hidden Shakespeare: *You see the Chinese Othello figure Flash cuts,* or *That's just a choreographed* Coriolanus *with a bit more blood.*

The ending Frankie gave each Flash video was pure Fong! Bruce Lee and Chuck Norris left piles of bodies behind. Frankie made customers out of both victims and villains. That's why I fell so hard for Frankie. He leveraged buyouts of silver linings to every sad sack's clouds.

We made love only after he'd rewound the tape. At forty-five, Frankie still had the Flash moves. And afterwards, we lay in bed and talked. Well, he talked; I mostly listened. I'm a good listener, the best. I know to pay attention. It makes the talker feel good, and all the while I'm filing away factoids for future use. Autodidacts are the best educated. I don't mean to knock my SUNY marketing degree—it should get a twenty-three-year-old a job that pays more than minimum wage, it cost Mama and Pappy enough—but classroom education isn't going to take anyone to the places that wisdom born of smarts will. I learned more in those two summer months in the cozy crook of Frankie's arm than in the four debt-loaded years on the Albany campus.

Before Frankie insinuated himself into my life, I'd convinced myself that I was just another restless upstate daughter looking to make it medium-big and marry medium-nice in Manhattan. In that Before Frankie epoch, I didn't read the papers or watch the news, but I knew, because all DiMartinos were Republicans, that the country had gone to the dogs, and the cities had been taken over by crack-cocaine addicts, rapists, muggers and welfare queens. Frankie changed all that. For Frankie, the New World was as green and crisp as a freshly counterfeited hundred-dollar bill. In the After Frankie months I became a news junkie, a fact hound. I started thinking like Frankie, a cornered rat with options. And suddenly life became interesting. Suddenly I was sniffing out possibilities where the world saw only problems.

About a month after we'd watched our first video together, as Frankie was slipping *Flash Takes All* into my rented recorder and explaining to me how the opening shot was his homage to "Les Demoiselles d'Avignon," I whispered a confession. "I wish I'd had the Flash for a dad," I said.

Pappy, forgive me; you aren't the one I regret.

Frankie inhabits a Frankie-centric universe. "Think lover, not father," he sulked. "Age doesn't diminish . . . uh, drive and virility."

Watch out, all you tigers and rhinos, I thought: the Flash would wipe out whole continents if he decided he was slipping. I hit the EJECT button on the VCR. "I wasn't talking about us, Frankie."

He pulled a tiny snapshot out of his snakeskin wallet and shoved it in my face. "The chap look old to you, dahling?"

I caught a smoky blur of a smiling Chinese face above a satin jacket, and lied, no. Not that the man looked old and droopy, not exactly. He looked more plumped up, embalmed.

"My dad," Frankie said. "At eighty-two."

"So this is where you get your good looks."

"Old age runs with its tail between its legs when it comes up against Fong genes." He didn't smile when he said this. "Genes count."

I grabbed Al's photo before Frankie could put it back in his wallet.

"What can you tell me about Bombay?" I asked that night, after we'd made love. "What do you know about Devigaon village?"

Hot, dry, smoky, full of whores: that's the litany I expected. But Frankie said nothing, he just stared. He stared at me the way I must have stared at him that first time.

"You're from there, aren't you?"

And I knew, from that instant, I had power over him. I was what he wanted, what he aspired to, and could never have. And I'd revealed it all to him, so casually, almost carelessly.

"That's it!" Frankie snapped his fingers. "I *knew* there was something exotic about you. A touch of Merle Oberon."

I didn't go to foreign movies, didn't know the names of foreign stars. From the way he said it, I assumed he was paying me a compliment.

"It's your eyes," he went on. "It's the way you walk. Like women in Burma balancing jugs on their heads . . ."

"Hey," I objected, "I don't do jugs!" I didn't give a damn about what women in Burma wore for hats. "I'm adopted." My voice sounded firmer, bolder, the second time. Not *I was adopted*, but *I am adopted*, meaning I want you to know that we've both invented ourselves, you couldn't have found another woman as much like you as I am if you'd taken out personals.

That night what must have started out for Frankie as a one-night stand clotted into codependency.

The not-quite-American playboy had plans on a grand scale for the not-quite-Asian novice playgirl. He wanted me to model for Chinese couturiers in Paris and London; to travel with him as his personal assistant to Honolulu for an FHP Board of Directors meeting. I could be the Elastonomics Girl, I could do half-hour infomercials.

"Trust me, my lovely little foundling," he said. "A new Hollywood star has to be made, not born." Blondes were dead; they'd been sent to rerun hell. My un-beach-bunny look was what California was dying for but didn't know yet. He got so carried away with the plans that he decided he'd make a new Flash movie, costarring me as an orphan who looks for, and with kick-boxing help finds, her long-lost parents. "The world'll fall in love with you!" he promised.

"What do you mean, Frankie?" I didn't need the world to fall in love with me.

"We'll call it *Farewell, My Fond Foundling*," he shouted. "That's it!"

And later that night, Frankie confided in me his dreams of the Fong Empire he would build by catering to American wants with Asian needs. Chinese need rhinoceros horns and tiger bones and prostitutes for potency. Americans want potency too, but they have to call it love, and they'll settle for Elastonomics to bring them both.

Americans convert needs into wants; Asians wants into needs. That was Frankie's point. It made enough sense. "So when I'm saying Elastonomics on the phone, I'm really saying tiger balls?"

"Absolutely." He stroked my cheeks, my throat, my collarbone. "I want to hear tiger balls and rhino horn in everything you say."

"Grrr, Mr. Elastonomics."

He called me Tiger from that night on.

Frankie Fong was my first mature lover, the first one I didn't need to get drunk to do it with, my first older-but-shorter man, my first non-Italian, nonclassmate hunk, but that doesn't explain mesmerism. I didn't want to manipulate him, like poor old Wyatt. I was putty for him. The charm of Frankie Fong started out as the charm of foreignness, of a continent I couldn't claim but which threatened to claim me. It ended up the opposite.

If it had all gone right in those hot last two weeks of August, if Frankie had been genuinely impulsive and asked me to marry him, I would have. Even if he'd just kept me around as his upstate concubine (delicious word), I'd have accepted. I'd have adjusted to his gifts of jade brooches and coral bracelets ("trinkets of value," he called them, "sew them into your suitcase"). And when the good feelings ran out, I'd have left him so he wouldn't have to leave me. I am not a jealous person. Whatever I did to Frankie or to others, jealousy was never my motive.

What I did was torch Frankie's precious home in Saratoga Springs. Flippant Frankie was right: there are only two categories of people, those with *wants*, and those with *needs*.

Baby Fong dropped out of the plump, drizzly sky one late-August afternoon in Saratoga Springs. What other reason besides a malevolent deity, or the supreme indifference of fate, could have compelled her to dump the semicomatose Aloysius in the care of smuggled-in, illiterate live-ins from Nanjing, ride the Amtrak to Troy, then rent a balloon from a Saratoga company called Bubbly in the Breeze, Inc.?

When I say "dropped," I mean "dropped." Baby's balloon landed between a row of rose bushes and a bed of Japanese irises in the backyard Frankie'd just had professionally landscaped. He said, "Why couldn't my mother have been another Imelda Marcos?" Why couldn't she spike-heel up and down Madison Avenue, dropping platinum-colored plastic?

Frankie's nickname for his mother was First Class Fong. Baby was a compulsive shopper with only one criterion. "You sure it real fine? You sure it genuine classy?" He'd caught her once in Singapore asking, "Is this your top price?" She could be on the Ginza or in Rome or in Toronto and she'd ask, "You sure this first-class stuff?" Why, oh why, Frankie grumbled, did he have to suffer for her obsessive need for "first-class" society? And why did she have to express it upstate by out-hosting Mary Lou Whitney?

I kept a file of First Class places, little crumbs of information from Frankie's ranting. Hazelton Lanes, Via Veneto, Union Square. The factoid I didn't have to file for keeps: Frankie ♥s Debby.

Saratoga Springs in the racing season attracts blue bloods and grifters, touts and tarts, writers, Degas wannabes, balletomanes and a real dog pound of high-class mutts. Baby confused the classiest riffraff with the classiest elite. She planned pageants instead of parties: Mongolian contortionists and Chinatown acrobats entertaining titled guests in striped tents; Chinese "boat people" in chef's hats wokking whole carp that they'd carried up from Chinatown on Amtrak wrapped in newspaper on their laps; Thai masseuses offering fussy cocktails from silver trays.

He didn't show up for a week. He couriered me gifts, mostly the unimaginative kind, like flowers, boxed candies, perfume and lingerie. And one expensive one: a black silk Chinese-y dress with long side slits. So, he wanted me to be more Chinese. I'd be more Chinese than the Great Wall. Frankie liked to buy flowers more than I liked to receive them, and as for chocolate, you can't sew it into the bottom of your suitcase. The dress I tried on. It looked okay on me. I had the mystery genes, the boyish hips and good legs. On Angie or cousin Nicole with their chunky bodies, the slits would've buckled out. They would've looked sluttish. Or, worse, pathetic.

The Saturday night of that dinner meeting with Baby, Frankie came over a half hour earlier than we'd arranged. I'd been ready and dressed for at least an hour: hair blow-dried wild, cheeks blush-brushed vampy, boyish body glamoured up in that Chinese sheath.

Before he could close the door behind him, I did a twirl and two-step to show off the whole getup.

"Nice," he said.

"Nice?" He made it sound like I'd just won the Miss Congeniality Contest in the Saratoga County Beauty Pageant.

"Very nice?"

Third runner-up for Miss Nassau County. "Frankie . . . ?" I went. "You want me to do something different with my hair? Don't I look okay?"

"Very nice."

"Jeesus, Frankie . . . nice? Like Merle What's-Her-Face nice?"

He focused on my shoes. Retro platforms in chartreuse patent leather.

"Too tacky?"

He was headed for my closet.

"Go ahead. Be my guest." I did have a quiet pair of black pumps. "I want to knock First Class Fong on her ass."

"I don't."

Frankie picked out a white silk shirt and a navy skirt and navy slingbacks. With a few grunted curses and twenty minutes of frowns and finger snapping, he made me over from in-your-face vamp to staid-on-the-outside, sultry-on-the-inside secretarial assistant. He slicked my thick hair down with gel and pinned it up in a neat roll. He lightened the blush and the eyeshadow, but plumped up my lips to a lotus pout. In the back of the closet he found a tan faux-croc pocketbook with a metallic shoulder chain.

"Voilà!" he whispered when he had adjusted the links for the pocketbook to hang just right against midhip. "Perfect! Smashing!"

I looked in the spotty, thrift-store mirror above the mantel. Frankie had paled down my eyes, brows, cheeks, but given them clarity. I had dared to cast myself as mysterious, I'd thought I was playing in Frankie's league, and he'd bounced me back to upstate reality. Clarity was the bond of give-and-take between us. Clarity, not love.

He scoured my drawers for accessories, and came up with a shirt length of emerald silk, which he draped like a shawl around my shoulders. "What do you think?"

"Do I need it?" DiMartinos do their thing with scarves. Shawls are exotic.

Frankie twitched the silk piece this way and that for the right effect. "Green looks good on you. When you walk in, have the bloody thing frame your shoulders just like that," he advised my speckled reflection in the mirror. "When you settle into your chair at the table, let it glide down on its own. You're not thinking about clothes, that's the main idea."

Because I'm thinking "Expiration date"? And what's he thinking? Rhino horns and tiger balls?

"Well," he said, giving me the final once-over, "it's in your hands now."

I caught the kiss he air-blew.

Frankie slapped his pockets for a pack of cigarettes. "Shit! I'm all out. Meet me at L'Auberge? We shouldn't both be late!"

It's in your hands now. I'd believed Frankie then. Maybe I still do. Success or failure'd been in my hands that evening. But the question I can't stop asking myself is, How had these hands come to belong to a DiMartino woman?

An orphan doesn't know how to ask, afraid of answers, and hopes instead for revelation. Ignorance isn't bliss, but it keeps risky knowledge at bay. I never badgered Mama to tell me all she knew about my toddler days. Mama must have liked it that way too. She kept my origins simple: hippie backpacker from Fresno and Eurasian loverboy, both into smoking, dealing and stealing. She left my bio data minimal: some sort of police trouble my hippie birth mother had got herself into meant that the Gray Nuns in Devigaon village had had to take me in; one of the nuns had renamed me Faustine after a typhoon, but Mama'd changed it officially to Debby after Debbie Reynolds, her all-time favorite.

It *was* in my hands. I didn't want it to be in anyone else's. This was a night I expected revelations. It would close on champagne and Frankie's saying, one hand on mine, another on Baby's, "Mama, she is the most important person in my life."

I was demanding acknowledgment, not a wedding ring.

Frankie slipped out of the apartment. I didn't stop him. From my window I heard Frankie slam the building's outer door, then slip into his Flash walk, swiveling and strutting through the parking lot, leap into a silver Jaguar I didn't know he owned and vanish around the block. I stayed at the window awhile, savoring the splintery roughness of the window frame, and the play of shadows cutting across the sidewalk. In the park the Dixieland band was doing a halfhearted job, but, thinking *Tonight's the big night, tonight Prince Flash will fit the glass slipper on the Foundling's foot,* I didn't mind at all.

By the time I made my teetery way on the slingbacks with the high heels and the pointy toes, an upscale crowd in a party mood was already clotting the sidewalk outside L'Auberge Phila, and the small open space around the bar, waiting for the maître d' to find them tables. My mood was good to begin with, but the head turns and near leers from tanned guys in summer blazers as I cut through the crowd to the maître d' made it soar.

"I'm with the Fong party," I announced. For the rest of my life: *The Fong party. Debby Fong.*

"Ah, yes, the others are waiting for you," the maître d' said with a perfunctory dip from the waist, and led me to a table for four. *See how they scrape!*

Frankie was in one of the two chairs that faced the wall. He was leaning forward, elbows on the tablecloth, listening to a young and very sexy Asian woman with long-lashed eyes and long black hair tell what must have been a joke. If this was Baby, then Baby was aptly named. She had a high, melodious voice, and she was saying, in an accent that sounded very much like Frankie's had when he'd called me that first night from Kuala Lumpur or wherever, "There was a talking bird in a golden cage stranded with a deaf-and-dumb chap on a desert island . . ." I stopped behind Frankie's chair, wanting to shout at Miss Asian Knockout: Hey, you can't call a person *dumb.* Not in Saratoga. I confidently waited for Frankie to feel my presence before I spoke up, but he just hung on her every word, looking down her dress.

"Hi!" I announced myself while the maître d' hovered.

Frankie scraped his chair back, and half rose to greet me, while the woman made a gesture with her hand that could have meant "Hello" or "Go away, don't bother us." The hand she waved was elegant: beautiful skin and delicate bones, set off by two large rings, one a huge black pearl and the other a heart-shaped sapphire. Asians must make the best "hands" models.

Another Asian woman, shorter and older, and dressed in a Chanel suit, joined us. She held her hand out straight, each finger stiff with rings. "Ah, you must have walked in while I was in the loo!" She had a pale oval face powdered paler, and vigilant eyes under green-shadowed lids. Her scalp showed through her thin hair, but what hair there was was dyed a dead black. "That's the trouble with middle age," she rattled on in her loud, good-humored voice. "Bladder ruins welcomes you've planned to the last detail. Oh, you wouldn't know, but you will. Where's that darn gift? Frankie's sung your praises, Miss DiMartino, hasn't he, Ovidia? We have a present for you. But first I have to scoot around Frankie and find it in one of the shopping bags behind my chair. I know you must be in a rush to get away from the boss, Frankie's such a slave driver, but it won't take me a mo. Frankie, do they have that first-class champagne I like? Have you asked the waiter?"

Ovidia stooped to rummage through the shopping bags at her feet. Frankie's eyes followed. I caught Ovidia's smile as she became aware of Frankie's interest.

"Look in the Harrods sack, dear," Mrs. Fong encouraged.

"That's a pretty necklace," Frankie muttered, his eyes on the pendant of pearls hanging from a gold chain just above Ovidia's modest cleavage.

"I'll tell you what we brought you, Miss Di. You don't mind if I shorten your name to Miss Di, names are so difficult. Anyway, if you're like Cynthia, that wonderful girl Frankie's got in KL, you probably hate surprises. Am I right?"

"Frankie?" Let my mean fears be unjustified, I prayed.

Ovidia straightened up just then. She held a prettily wrapped medium-sized box out to Baby, for Baby to hand in turn to me I guessed, but it was Frankie, and only Frankie, she was looking at.

"Not that one," Baby said.

"Frankie?" I tried again.

He smiled at Ovidia for a very long moment, then turned away, picked up the wine list. It hit me, like a mugger's truncheon from behind on prime-time TV police shows: Frankie'd presented me to First Class Fong as a simple Saratoga secretary.

"A handbag," Baby stage-whispered, "because nobody doesn't not have an use for a handbag, am I right?"

Ovidia pulled out my present from the Harrods shopping sack. It wasn't gift-wrapped. And it wasn't a pocketbook. "Here we are," she announced.

Ovidia's pretty hand was still dangling the Singapore Airlines freebie toilet kit as I ran to the entrance, and up Phila Street.

"Lousy day at the tracks? Something a drink can fix?" someone said in a nothing-to-lose voice. I kept running.

I had to nuke Frankie from my memory. No such person as Frankie, never had been a Frankie, no supercool superrich Asian lover who opened up a whole continent for me. I'd made him up out of needs I didn't know I had. It suddenly came to me as I sat in the car why First Class Fong had dropped herself into my life. Oh Baby, thank you. You brought me more than the freebie toilet bag. If Wyatt's vision for me was right, I'd be able to pay my own first-class Singapore Airlines fare, and buy a Saratoga apartment. One day I'd be tall, pretty, rich, a mover and shaker as long as I knew enough to lie low on bad days and scratch my fleas in private, right? Tomorrow I'll wake up with a cold nose and bright eyes and the first rich couple with a big yard that comes in will take me home.

No more rhino horns and tiger balls, think Animal Shelter. Wyatt gave me a base to build from. He didn't realize that a few of us are given chance after chance because we have life after life to get it right. In fact, I wouldn't mind another couple of chances with Wyatt now that I am not a stubby, punk thirteen. One thing Wyatt got totally wrong: cuteness counts for some, but not for all. You get put down when you finally run out of wrath and a canny sense of timing.

I drove straight to the pound. It was minutes to closing time, and the dogs mostly lay curled tight in their roomy cages, their backs pressed against the grille.

"They look so sad," I remarked to the Animal Shelter officer, a woman in her fifties. She was nursing a sick iguana, which she cradled against her chest as if it were a baby. "Do they sense time is ticking?"

"Oh, they've just had a big supper," she said, without taking her eyes off the iguana. "And they're probably worn out from the good run they got today. We have a new volunteer this week, a high school kid who wants to study veterinary medicine. A really sweet kid whose Lab just died of diabetes." She stroked the iguana. "Sniffles getting you down, Izzy?"

"Mind if I take a quick look around?" I asked the officer.

"Sure thing," she said. "Glad for interest, glad for company. The cats are in the last two stalls, all the way down the hall behind that door and to the left. Be a big boy now, Izzy, don't fight the medicine. Are you looking for a dog or for a kitty?"

"I'm not sure," I lied. "Probably a dog."

"Take your time," the officer advised. "It never works when you choose on impulse. Not for you, and certainly not for the dog. Best to think through all the stuff like what breed's best for your family, do you have babies, do you live in a big house or a tiny apartment, will your neighbors complain about barking. The big fellow in the first cage to the right as you go through that door was brought back last week. The man said his wife was afraid he'd trample the baby."

I walked in through the door marked ANIMALS & OTHERS, past Izzy's empty case and two glass cases of thin snakes, to where the dogs, cats, rabbits and ferrets were kept. That evening I counted seven dogs, though one of them had a NOT FOR ADOPTION sign above its cage.

The dog inside had a huge, grim head, and a don't-mess-with-me-and-mine kind of muscular face; in fact, it looked more like a wild bear than a housebroken pet. But its body was long, slender and elegant, stuck on top of twitchy little legs.

"See that head?" The officer lowered Izzy into its case, and whistled at the dog. The dog stared and stiffened its ears, but didn't scurry towards the grille.

"A dog with dignity," I commented. *No wants, no needs, no expiration date?*

"He's got a bit of Akita in him," the officer explained. "You can see it in the massive head."

"Akita?" Some fancy breed that nobody I knew owned.

"Poor fellow, he's also got some dachshund or poodle. Look at those matchstick legs."

"Why the sign?" I asked.

"He hasn't had all his shots yet. First we have to gauge if he has what it takes to be adopted."

"I'd consider it." It wasn't exactly a lie. Poor mutt. It was bred like me, with crossed signals and conflicting impulses.

"Wait till the end of the racing season," the officer advised. "That's when we get all the pets the summer folks don't want to take back home with them. You'd be surprised. Beginning of September's when I get really desperate for homes."

When I got back to my apartment, I found a half dozen gladiola stalks, the gift-wrapped box, which turned out to be a Chanel handbag, and a note from "Mr. Francis" on Elastonomics letterhead. The note was brief and word-processed. It said, *"C'est la vie.* Thanks for the superb times. I shall have left town on business by the time you get this. The apartment is yours gratis till the end of the month. Good luck and god bless."

"Why waste your money?" Mama sighed when I called her the next afternoon and told her that I'd just signed on as a client with Finders/Keepers, a family-reuniting service in Albany. "We're your family. Aren't we your family, Debby?"

"I need to know." I should've stopped there. I heard Mama's dishwasher going. She'd be in pull-on knit pants and a T-shirt, broken-down Wallabees, a bandana tied low over her forehead, cleaning up after making her nectarine relish, which Pappy never dared tell her he hated. Family secrets. "About crossed signals and conflicting impulses. They say there's a time every adopted kid suddenly has to know."

Mama chose innocence. "Didn't it work out with that nice Oriental man?"

"I don't know any nice men. Apart from Pappy, of course."

"Pappy's going fishing this weekend. With Uncle Benny. He needs the break. They both need a break. Benny got hit bad in that malpractice suit. Pappy's advising bankruptcy. You'd've thought chiropractors were safe."

"Mama, I need to know what you know."

"Hold on a minute. I need to sit, and the cord doesn't stretch far enough. Let me pull up a stool."

"I know what to get you for Christmas," I joked. "A cordless." I heard Mama's heavy tread on the kitchen's old wooden floor, and Patsy Cline on tape. Then the dragging sound of the stool.

When she came back on the phone, she asked, "How much will you have to shell out, Debby?"

In blood or cash, Mama?

"They might be dead, hon. I'm sorry, I didn't mean for it to come out that way."

"Don't be sorry, Mama." For all I knew, Finders/Keepers was a scam, the kind that's exposed on *Dateline* or *60 Minutes*. "We have a name at least."

Mama sobbed. "Why, Debby? What didn't we do?"

"It's not about us." I loved this woman, but love wasn't enough in the face of need; it would never be. Need teased out the part of me that the orphanage had whited-out in my best interest. "It's about me and them."

"We don't have a name, hon, we have a confused kid turned hippie. What kind of a real last name is Iris-Daughter?"

"I'll find out soon enough."

"There's not much to find, Deb. The nuns weren't great at paperwork."

"I don't have a choice, Mama."

"Some of the documents were sealed. I'm pretty sure that's what our lawyer and the orphanage's lawyers said. Because of the lawsuit."

"What lawsuit?"

"Oh, nothing to do with us, dear. Indians were pressing those charges. The Indian government."

"What charges?"

"I'm not sure what exactly. But serious charges."

"That's a break for me, Mama. If they had a police record, that's something to go on."

"Being a criminal is a break? What kind of talk is that?"

"Just kidding, Mama. You brought me up to be decent."

"Do you want to come to dinner Friday night? Sleep over? Pappy'll be gone. I have a nice pork roast in the freezer."

"Can't. Sorry. Something I have to do this Friday." I made my mind up what that something was the moment I finished lying to Mama.

"Well, there wouldn't have been much more to tell you in person, I guess. Our lawyer said the one thing we had in our favor was that the woman was an American citizen. That made you a citizen too. The woman told the nuns she'd sign the adoption papers if they got us to pay her airfare back to the States."

"So you saw her?"

"No, she had us buy a Delhi–San Francisco ticket. We didn't want to see her. We wanted to give you a clean start, that's why we changed the name the nuns gave . . ."

"Faustine?"

"It sounded so foreign. Fossteen. Why're you doing this now, Debby? You didn't show the least curiosity before, you never asked questions . . ."

"It's not because I miss them, Mama. It's about medical history." And psychic legacies.

I hadn't yet met Madame Kezarina, the pay-per-prediction prophet with unusual props. I hadn't yet stuck voodoo pins into her Hate-Me Hand nor rubbed the big toe of her bronze Vishnu Foot for good luck. I hadn't sat under Madame K's Mariposa Mystic, a wooden doll bought on sale at a Taxco boutique, and meditated on genetic mysteries. The mariposa is a butterfly-woman with horns and wings in dramatic reds, blues and greens, with big-nippled breasts and larva legs and feet. She hangs on the wall of Madame K's "office," a bug evolving into deity, a deity dissolving into bug. I see myself in the mariposa doll. Just as I had in the freakish dog in the pound.

Finders/Keepers took my fee and told me to get in touch with its San Francisco office, which would be in a better position than the Albany office to help. My file had been electronically transferred. I wouldn't have to pay new start-up charges, though the hourly rates might be a little higher out west. The California bug in my head, I followed my file; I fulfilled my fate.

But before I got in my car to track down Clear Water Iris-Daughter, whatever her current name, on the other side of the continent, I made sure the bad times I'd pledged did indeed roll Francis Albert Fong's way. One late-August night, I stood with gawkers across from the turreted and gargoyled Fong house on Union Avenue and watched rivers of flame lick at vintage velvet drapes, then split off and multiply, and crawl like amoebas across massive oak doors and curved-glass windows. A spectacular extravaganza of light, sound, heat. I was an auteur, too. Frankie had no right to be angry. He had a duty to take pride in my accomplishment.

Clarity. That's what I prize more than knowledge. In the hot, harsh light of clarity I saw for myself the difference between justice and vengeance.

Frankie would file an inflated insurance claim. That was okay with me; the Flash's losses deserved some extra compensation from corporate thugs. The costs I extracted— loss of past and loss of pride—were unreimbursable, and permanent. Frankie wouldn't pursue any case of arson. He couldn't afford to invite too much investigation, not with the undocumented Chinese aliens in his basement, the ones who did the cooking and cleaning for First Class Fong. The Fong Home Products frontman would hire new waifs and run them through mock interviews in other motels. And maybe get lucky next time.

Inner peace. That's what I gained that smoky summer night as a wide, gracious porch smoldered and Frankie wept. *Nirvana is finding the tiger balls within you.* I ambled to the used Corolla Pappy and Mama bought me for graduation, and I made my sputtery getaway while the firefighters were still hacking away at Frankie's dream house with their axes.

Part Two

Eastern, Central, Mountain, I ate the zones a day at a time, Chicago to Cheyenne to Salt Lake and Reno. For twenty years I'd set my watch back and forward twice a year, now I was turning it back every day. It seemed like a gift from God, that extra hour, then two, then three—no wonder Californians were different; they had more daylight to do things, longer nights to sleep through. That went a long way to explain the difference between Serena DiMartino and Clear Water Iris-Daughter.

Like Columbus, I was on the Pacific glidepath looking for the westward passage. Out west, prime time must start in the afternoon. Letterman was already back home in Connecticut when he was just starting in California. Weirdness.

Before that week I'd never been west of Niagara Falls; now I was driving through places that were only rumors. States no DiMartino had ever been in or talked about kept taking me by surprise: Ohio? Indiana? *So that's where they put it!* I'd never thought there could be so much emptiness, and so many places just like Schenectady with their own evening news, with their own traffic jams and freeways. I didn't get it. Why would people choose to live there?

My first antelope. My first Indian. First real mountains, with August snow. Radio signals from every state west of the Rockies, south of Alaska and north of the Canal filled my ears with strange music and revival and call-in complaints. At night, all Spanish. I didn't see a tree for two days, and then came the downscale sublime *Utah!* The state had an exclamation point on its license plates like it was its own musical. Seven brides for one horny brother? Salt flats, miles in every direction, which I walked on, fell down on and stuck my tongue on, *Hey, where's the ketchup? You shoulda seen that French fry!* I bet myself the next state had to be California because my money was thin by then, but it turned out to be Nevada, even drier and emptier, where gas stations and 7-Elevens had slot machines and "ranch" meant "whorehouse," which I discovered when I drove into one looking for cowboys. Probably lots of those cowgirls working the ranches had more than arson in their pasts. I made forty dollars on the slots crossing the state.

California sure knew how to make an entrance, knew how to keep you waiting. Forget and forgive the stuff they taught in school about the Donner Pass.

After all the dust and emptiness, I was primed.

You are a twenty-three-year-old SWF, I tested myself. *You are attractive, and you are street-smart in a Schenectady/Albany sort of way. You have a sense of humor, which gets you dates and jobs. You also have your pride, which, when it gets out of hand, burns down an ex-boyfriend's house. Given such assets of your looks and character and the liability of your situation, do you:*

A. hide out on a Nevada ranch and save your neck until Flash calls off his goon squad?

B. become a Mormon and save your soul?

C. enlist in the Peace Corps and save the world?

D. confront your deadbeat mom?

Luv ya, California! Greetings from Debby Clearwater-Daughter!

I owed it to my family to share my happiness. On an impulse I got off the highway, and from the pay phone of the gas station closest to the exit ramp, I dialed Mama. The phone rang and rang. Pappy didn't believe in answering machines. So I dialed Angie next. Some jazz group I didn't recognize came on first, then a man with a whispery voice and an accent I couldn't place. "You have reached the pad of Egberto and the *bella* Angela. When two people are in love, answering your call is not a top priority. Leave a message or get a life. Whatever you decide, you have thirty seconds. Oh, and Beth, Ingrid and Manju have moved on to Alberta and couldn't care less about messages."

I slapped the pay phone a couple of times with the heel of my palm.

The teenaged attendant shook his head. "I know just how you feel," he said. "Sometimes that phone don't work so good."

I caught the spaced-out smile on his bronzed, benign face. A good mood is a good mood, even when chemically induced. I envied him. I said, as a joke, "Think I should sue the phone company?"

"Why not?" the kid said. He picked a stick of beef jerky out of a jar by the cash register, and peeled its wrap partway. "What do you have to lose? Time's running out on corporate deep pockets."

"My sister," I volunteered, "wants me to get a life."

The kid took a meditative chew. "Cool," he said.

"My first time in California, would you believe?"

He pulled another vile-looking stick out of the beef jerky container. "Hey, on the house," he said. "Have a nice life. Have a nice day the rest of the day."

I sucked and chewed on the jerky as I got back on the highway. If the world has a finite supply of bad days and nice days, I owed it to myself to grab as many nice ones as I could. Go for bliss. Dump pain, pity and rage on somebody else. Pursue happiness: that's the American way. Dial the Bay Area branch of Finders/Keepers the next chance you get. Muddy Clear Water's conscience. Or, better still, make Bio-Mama pay for her shallow-pocketed maternalness.

And when getting a life is your goal, why put off till tomorrow what you can do this nanosecond?

Pursuing bliss, I took the very next exit ramp off the highway, and called San Francisco information for Finders/Keepers. "Nothing under that name," the operator said.

"Maybe I'm spelling it wrong," I pleaded, "anything under *Ph* instead of *F, Qu* instead of *K?*"

"I don't show anything, ma'am. Check the spelling. Have a nice day."

Debby DiMartino died and Devi Dee birthed herself on the Donner Pass at the precise moment a top-down Spider Veloce with DEVI vanities (driver's blond hair billowing around a clamp of expensive speakers, cigarette cueing imaginary music) cut me off in front of the Welcome to California Fruit Inspection Barrier to take the only open slot.

Of course, the Fruit Inspector waved DEVI through and stopped my sensible Corolla with its New York nonvanities and went through its yeah-I-left-in-a-hurry-but-I'm-intending-to-stay-no-matter-what backseat jumble of clothes, cardboard boxes, garbage sacks, CDs and tapes. The Fruit Buster sniffed for suspicious odors and pounced on a plastic Baggie I'd been spitting orange peels and tossing banana skins, crumpled tissues and candy wrappers into the last three days. I have a fast metabolism, and back in New York I'd have shriveled the Fruit Buster with a hey!-you-metabolism-chauvinist! glare, but at the California border I cringed.

I'm a disgrace to California, I deserve to be turned away. That was my last true Debby-thought, all wrapped up in ash, sackcloth and guilt.

"Okay, cool," the Fruit Buster waved me on, "I'll dump this stuff in the right recycling bins." He had two silver rings piercing his left ear rim, and an official cap perched on an explosion of black, bristly hair. He was Asian, but not Chinese. My time with Frankie and his Chinese-intensive labor force at FHP had made me intuitive about who wasn't Chinese. Chinese was just the beginning. Frankie got scary specific: Chinese out of Singapore, he'd pronounce; Malay Chinese. Filipino Chinese, Sumatran, Javan. The Fruit Inspector was American Chinese; he probably wouldn't have appreciated Frankie's detection skills.

I thanked the Inspector with smarmy gratitude, I was that touched by his laid-back California efficiency. I didn't forget that he'd treated me differently from the blond in the top-down Spider Veloce. Humiliation by the broccoli police didn't happen to blondes who lived inside their sound-designed universes, who ran through snow flurries with their long hair flying, whose cigarettes sent messages of assumed immortality. Of course I knew I'd been discriminated against, but nicely, so why not treat it as a learning experience? Hello California.

"Whoa, no problem. Have a nice life!" The cool Inspector launched a perfect jump shot. Old Baggie of trash and guilt disappeared into the Dumpster.

"Yo," I shouted back, "you too."

Reborn, admitted, launched into clean, conquerable gravity-free space. Even the air felt young, innocent, healthy. A few fat midsummer snowflakes danced like spit on a griddle off my Corolla's sizzling hood. Was it a cold day with warm sun, a New York April sort of day? Or upstate October, a warm day with icy winds?

Devi arm-wrestled Debby. I was quicker, stronger as Devi; my intuitions were sharper, my impulsiveness rowdier. As Devi, I came into possession of my mystery genes. Thank you, Clear Water. And you, too, thank you, "Asian National."

And thank you, Baby Fong, and what the heck, Frankie, too, for forcing me to deal with my not being a real DiMartino. Like Angie, or like cousin Nicole. Nicole graduated from Hudson Valley Community, and she's now assistant-producing for some crack-of-dawn cable channel and living with a painter in an illegally converted loft in West Chelsea. Nicole's a true DiMartino. She can afford to be hooked on Danielle Steele and fairy tales, because she has a family, because she has a family history that's corroborated by uncles, aunts, grandparents and cousins like Angie. She thinks of Cousin Gino, the only DiMartino who's done time in a state penitentiary, as Jesse James with a Sicilian twist. That's why I wouldn't share my stupid, sordid past as Faustine with someone whose only ambition was to move up to associate producer so she could get a taxi budget.

In my family, ambitious women my age went down to Manhattan to get a life. They always had, always would. Before August, before Frankie, I'd expected to head south, too, stake out sleeping-bag space on Angie's floor, be a dog walker for neighborhood gays, make contacts and get a break, find a job in something self-expressive like fashion or decor, where my height and voice would take me to the head of the line, scout an apartment-share I could afford and keep my eyes open for the Fabio of my daydreams. I'd expected to do all this out of desperation. Because I'd known that I didn't fit into Hudson Valley any more comfortably than I did into the Asia of hippie mothers and Catholic missionaries.

Blonde like the Spider Veloce blonde was doable, but not my style. I put my money on Wyatt's wish that someday soon I'd be rich and powerful as well as tall, pretty, free. The Golden State offered freaky-costumed freedom, and more; it offered immunity from past and future sins. Goodbye, Debby DiMartino. Long live Devi Dee.

So while I glide down I-80 from the thawing mountains past baking Sacramento to the perpetual spring of the Bay Area, while I negotiate the traffic surge of Berkeley and the Bay Bridge into San Francisco, while I count out traveler's checks from my emaciated hoard to pay for a cheap room in a Tenderloin hotel, let me tell you how I got over Frankie. In California, many men saw in me the telltale hint of Burmese schlepping water jugs on their heads.

Some days in Chinatown, strangers claimed me as a fellow-lost. In a Chinese restaurant while I was stoking up on the all-you-can-eat, a waiter mumbled something in a soft, gloomy voice, then hovered for an answer I couldn't give. In a McDonald's, an Indian man who looked like a student blurted to me, "Wanna catch a new Amitav?"

Deep down I envied the Chinese waiter and the Indian student. The guys were geeks, but they knew who they were. They knew what they'd inherited. They couldn't pass themselves off as anything else. No evasions, no speculations, no let's-pretends. They didn't see themselves as special or freakish.

The trouble was, I wasn't a geek, a freak, a weirdo. I'd had a life and the chance at a Big Life, and lost it, temporarily. I told myself, *For now why not be Devi the Ten-*

*derloin prowler, all allure and strength and zero inno-
cence, running away from shame, running to revenge?*

Who but a foundling has the moral right to seize not
just a city, but a neighborhood, and fashion a block or two
of it into home? When you inherit nothing, you are entitled to everything: that's the Devi Dee philosophy.

My Corolla became my boardinghouse after two expensive nights in the Tenderloin hotel owned by a Mrs.
Patel. Asia dogged me, enfolded me. Mrs. Patel's Asia
smelled of Lysol and rancid cooking oil. During the day I
scoured the city for a cheap room. I drove from Presidio
to Portrero, from Russian Hill to Hunter's Point, parking
the car whenever I liked a view or spotted a dog that
needed petting.

Oh, how the city seduced me! I thrilled to the skyline's
geometry. Rectangles, cylinders, rhomboids, pyramids: all
shapes belonged. And I loved San Francisco back, loved
its parks filled with lovers, sunbathers, Frisbee tossers,
loved its drowsy drunks let alone on streets, its nose-
ringed schoolboys riding public buses, its skinny gray
ridges stuck with pastel matchbox houses, its tangerine
Golden Gate and sailboats in the Bay, its streaky sunlight
on foggy days, its Day-Glo graffiti inside streetcar tunnels.
WE FUCK HOGS. DUNIA LOVES JORGE. BEAT SENSELESS. CEE-
DOUBLE-YOU. COPS WET THEIR PANTS.

I parked the car, and strode unfamiliar streets, tapping
businessmen for fives and tens, starting small by picking
up pennies and dimes, paying attention to the bases of
parking meters, then lifting wallets from too-tight jeans,

snatching purses off coffeehouse tables. The streets of California are paved with silver and papered in green; I could even stop for lattes when petty thievery made me thirsty. Some days I explored the city on borrowed bikes, the Dee System of pickup and delivery. This is the West, and I was claim jumping. From now on, life was a board game: Pass Go. Go to Jail. Looks and a body: that's a Get Out of Jail Free card.

It was the Haight I finally picked as my space. My space, my turf, my *homeland.* It was where I should have been born if the Fresno flower child had strayed no farther from home than Ashbury and Haight. But then I'd have had a different look and less curiosity about sex and transcendence. I'd have inherited the Haight Street I'll-cross-when-and-where-I-want-and-at-my-speed posture of entitlement. I had to practice a camel-like imperturbability as I crossed the streets on red, while motorists waited.

The Corolla-As-Motel-Room needed some getting used to. I wadded up dirty laundry to make myself a kind of sleeping pallet. For privacy I taped freebie weeklies to the windows. No cops hassled me, no creeps hustled me. What they said of the Haight, I mean the historical epoch, the mood I'd missed, I mean my bio-mom's times and wants and needs and not the place, was still true. Do your own thing, do it proudly, and no one will bother you. Feel free, and you *shall* be free. I was a Cowbabe in Goodwill chaps riding a Japanese auto. Clear Water was never this free, this strong!

The car was room, and board came from neighborhood soup kitchens. Faustine and Debby were brought up Catholics, but Devi followed her nose: the Hare Krishnas, Buddhists, Baptists, Black Muslims and some religions that entwined love and profit, charity and sex, faith and ecology, space and time, combinations I hadn't stumbled upon upstate. At the Church of Divine Intergalactica, parishioners wore crowns of Viking horns and feathered headdresses, headgear meant to collect outer-space signals undetectable on normal wavelengths. I felt free; I was free. It just happened overnight; one day I was afraid and on the outside, the next day I was a kind of outlaw, on the side of other outlaws. Maybe I was programmed that way; it seemed totally natural to identify with dropouts, to step around cops, to look out for scanners and closed-circuit monitors. All that shrapnel on cherubic faces, all those brandings and tattoos, looked cool, though not for me. The Haight's lesson was: Nothing in appearance or behavior need cost a drop of dignity. I didn't look jobless and didn't feel homeless. No sour odor of dim futurity.

Stoop Man was the first neighborhood friend I made while I was scouting the city on my own for Bio-Mom. He had fruit and he shared it. We started with chatter about greenhouse gases and ozone layers. Stoop Man sat all day every day on the stoop of the triplex that housed the Church of Divine Intergalactica. He owned a set of seven signal-receiving headwear, one for each day of the week, Viking, Roman, Indian, Greek, Star Wars, biblical and Disney, all of them handcrafted from cardboard, velvet and tin.

One morning in late September, he stopped me with, "Did you feel that one, sugar?" He was sitting on the lowest step of the stoop as usual, but that day he touched my elbow. He was wearing my favorite, the Queen of Sheba tiara.

"Feel what?" I smiled at his fingers still on my arm.

The morning stayed bright, but all the car alarms were going off. Pigeons went into panic, and circled the telephone poles.

"The Earth move, what else? Sugar, your smile makes me feel good, and I haven't been feelin too good for a while, you know what I'm sayin? Girl, you try being the Sultan of Bosnia, just try it for a day, get all your horses shot up, get all your sheep and goats barbecued by infidels, and pretty soon you'll feel the way I do. Hungry and depressed, that's how. Famished, you know what I'm sayin? What you reckon they be servin up at the Hare Krishnas for lunch?"

Stoop Man became my ticket to soup kitchens. The street people accepted me as his girlfriend. That's how he introduced me. "Say hi to my girlfriend, she touched down from another planet." "Must have," they'd kid, "she hasn't the sense of an earthperson, that's for sure." The street people made room for me in soup lines. They tipped me off on which stores had hidden cameras, what time the Japanese and German tour buses came by ("The famous corner of Haight and Ashbury, the Cradle of Flower Power, ladies and gents") so that I could do a little camera posing, chant my down-on-my-luck or my what-a-shit-country-we-live-in sob story and squeeze wads of sympathy cash out of fat-cat tourists.

I made other friends, Duvet Man, who lived inside his goose-down quilt and managed to be at the head of every food line, and Tortilla Tim, who saved me from being knifed by a Mill Valley kid weirded out on crack, and a guy who reminded me of Wyatt. A lot of people reminded of people I'd known, like we'd all drifted west till we'd run out of land, and then'd started to mutate a little, like salmon on their way back to spawn, getting a little cruder, a little uglier, on the way to die. The guy who reminded me of Wyatt looked like Wyatt, and kind of talked like Wyatt, too. One time just as I was about to make a small buy, he hummed a warning from a doorway. "Neck size, narc disguised." I took him to the backseat of the Corolla that September night, and spilled my guts. I told him about Celia Montoya, the counseling Circle, the telemarketing job I'd left so I could find one or both my parents. The rest could wait.

"No parents? Some people have all the luck," he said. He pulled a roll of breath mints from his pocket. "The name's Gabe by the way, like the archangel."

"My name's Devi."

"Like the goddess, eh? I had to learn all that Hindu, Jain, Buddhist shit at the U of T."

"Where's that? Texas?"

"Toronto, Texas, Tulsa, Topeka, Tempe."

"Wow," I murmured. "A goddess!"

"Tampa, Toledo—you shouldn't need a private eye to track your Aged Ps." He laughed. "Not if you are a goddess."

"I was thinking of starting with the Yellow Pages."

"Eenie meenie minie mo, et cetera?"

"I was thinking I'd pick the very first or the very last name listed."

"Devi Aardvaark? Try Buzzards, Inc., in the Yellow Pages."

"Buzzard? Like the bird?"

"If they ask, say Gabriel referred you. As in the archangel."

We hung together the next couple of days, not doing much, just staking out a square of sidewalk at the corner of Belvedere and Haight, holding up a sign, A BUCK FOR AN ANGEL OR A GODDESS, YOU NEVER KNOW, feeling good about the world, especially good about the dollar bills we collected, and then Gabe took off with the sign and the cash. He stuck a note on my windshield. *Hope the PIs can help. Wish we'd met earlier. Just too fucked up.*

I looked for Buzzards, Inc., in the Yellow Pages. No Buzzards, but there was a listing for Vulture, Inc. I called and left my name on tape, then realized that I had no phone number for them to call me back at, so I hung up. Next I looked up the Church of Divine Intergalactica in the phone book. The Stoop Man's church was listed under *D*, as Divine Intergalactica Worship Facility. I called Vulture, Inc., back, and this time left the DIWF number on the agency's answering machine.

A whole week went by without any calls for me at the Stoop Man's. I called the Vulture, Inc., number again, and kept calling until a human voice answered. "It's Devi Dee again" was all I got in before the voice, a man's, barked, "No solicitations, no market research surveys, no interest in freebie cruises or other prizes, so goodbye and thanks."

"And fuck you, too," I muttered to the dead line.

"All worked up, Goddess?" The Stoop Man snuck up on me on the sidewalk. He had on a beat-up, collapsible top hat and a satin-lined cape.

"Is that what they're calling me on the street? I'll kill Gabe!"

"Whoa! Bad nerves! You need something potent."

"So what're you selling?"

"Not selling. I'm giving it away today. The abracadabra of happiness."

"In pill, powder or vial?"

"All of the above." He flapped his cape, while he tap-danced in his running shoes. "Works like magic. How do you want it, Goddess?"

"I don't need magic," I grumbled. "I need a detective."

Very early the next morning, while I was still asleep in my Corolla parked under a pigeon-free tree on a fogged-up block just south of Haight Street, a film company showed up with a convoy of trailers. Frankie never told me what bullies film crews on location are. They push real people from their homes on real streets and think you'll be happy being a part of some fantasy you'll never see. This film crew operated as though location shooting were military conquest. Longhaired guys rang doorbells and ordered sleepy car owners to please move their cars because the film company had paid the city for permits to park their semis and their Range Rovers instead. They told store owners not to open, people not to come out until the all clear was sounded. Funky young assistants put up police barricades. A smart aleck rapped on my papered-over back window. "Hey, man, time to haul ass," he commanded in his mellow way.

I stepped out of the Corolla. Stoop Man, Duvet Man, Tortilla Tim, Beamer Bob, Snorting Sam, Pammy Whammy, everyone in the neighborhood, were already gathered behind one of the barricades on the far sidewalk. They weren't looking my way; they were interested in the food table. The laggards, people I recognized from soup lines and doorways, were being encouraged by a woman in purple tights and yellow tank top to drag themselves and their supermarket carts and their milk crates and garbage sacks out of the crew's way.

The woman fixed a friendly eye on me. "Hi, need help moving your car?"

"Who do you think you are?" I said.

"Locations PA," she said. "We do have the city's permission, you know."

I held my hand out. "Devi," I announced. "Also known as Goddess."

The woman gave my fingers an air-shake. "We need you to cooperate."

"Why?"

"Hey, nothing personal." She flashed a tense smile. Her lips had been given a collagen workout. "The city permit—"

"You don't have a permit from me," I interrupted.

"That's true"—the woman backed away from me— "very true." She signaled the tow truck I hadn't noticed before, because it was parked around the corner. "Look, I don't make the rules. I'm not the bad guy here."

My fists clenched up on their own. "Well, I do! I make the rules! So beat it, Ms. Loc!"

The woman looked down at her shoes. They were Mary Janes in purple suede. I began to enjoy myself. *PA ponders power play versus penitence.* I could still miss Frankie at the strangest times.

"Look, could you like move your car out of here for now, and maybe, like take it up with the mayor or something?" She sent an anxious glance to where Stoop Man was lecturing a longhaired man. "Ham?" she spoke into her walkie-talkie.

The longhaired man raised a walkie-talkie to his lips. "I just learned about inner-city problems in other solar systems. This dude's a perfect extra. See if you can get me Sarah. Or any of the casting munchkins."

"Ham," the locations PA pleaded, "can you spare a minute? We have a situation."

The man with the gray hair to his shoulders had to be in production. Some sort of desk job in the entertainment business, anyway. He wasn't crew, and he wasn't talent. I Sherlocked that from his clothes: a dress shirt and tuxedo jacket, white slacks, white loafers, pale panama hat on an oversized head. The white slacks had double pleats, the loafers gilt buckles that didn't glint in the sun. Pretty cool himself. Not too many guys can wear white shoes and white slacks with wit or style. The shirt was authentic Jazz Age twenties, not shopping-mall knockoff. I'd worked at the expensive Love at Second Site too many summers in Saratoga not to know vintage from junk. Smooth, I decided.

Ham maneuvered Stoop Man behind the police lines, then ambled to where I was giving his assistant a hard time, all the while nodding to gawkers and shaking hands. Money changing hands as Ham advanced. He didn't doff his panama, but he did scoop up my left hand in both his and kiss the inside of my wrist.

"Hi, honey, I'm Ham." He hung on to my hand, and gave me a deep, I-really-care-about-you look. "What's the problem? How can I help?"

"For starters, get this dodo out of my face."

Ham did, with an "I'll take care of this, Mimi, but have Sam call my office and check for messages; I hope Arturo made his flight okay."

"Good luck," the PA said over her shoulder.

Ham glanced at Pammy Whammy. She was at the crafts-service table, flirting with a man wearing some sort of utility belt. The man was more interested in her than in the Danish in his hand.

"You looking to break into movies like everyone else?" Ham asked. "You want it, you got it. The usual rate. Fifty bucks cash for the day."

"So that's how you guys take care of problems?"

"That's the rate," Ham repeated. "Nonunion nonfeatured extra." He leaned towards me. I felt my back press against the Corolla's door. Dawn had started out foggy, and the car was more soaked than dewy. "Are we working it out?"

I sized up my advantage. "What is this shit?" I snapped. "Ethnic cleansing?"

"That's pretty heavy, honey."

"Well, here's a counteroffer." I slipped my hand out of his, reached in through the driver's side window and pressed the horn and kept pressing it and let up only when he pleaded, "Okay, LA tactics always win. So how much are we talking? Are you the community rep or just acting freelance?"

I tried to think big. "A grand," I blurted. "In cash. No deductions."

Ham's face relaxed. "You got it." He laughed.

I cursed myself for thinking small-time Hudson Valley.

Ham consolidated his win. "That's you plural. You as spokesperson of, and disburser for . . ."

I was a counterfeit wheeler-dealer. Ham was the genuine thing.

"What's your community organization? My assistant'll need a name."

I thought he was going to call me on the scam. But he smiled instead, as though he and I were playing a game.

"Have your assistant phone me." I pointed to the pay phone.

"You have to come up with just the right name," he advised. "Names count. How about Lower Haight Development Authority, or—"

I cut him off. "I hate authority. Development Association." Ham looked impressed. He lifted his panama and dipped from the waist in a Japanese bow. I had a good thing going. "And what's this Upper and Lower Haight bit, elitist scum! We're the HDA. Your office is dealing with the HDA."

Ham made a note on his palm with a Mont Blanc ballpoint. "My office, tomorrow. Be there?" He pulled a business card out of the pocket of his dress shirt.

"You've done this before, haven't you?"

"I'd guess so have you, honey."

I flicked the card in through the car window. "Why should I trust you, Mr. Ham?"

The man acted stunned. Finally he said, "You have a sense of humor."

"What's the joke?"

"I'm Ham," the man said. "Because I'm Ham, Hamilton Cohan. *The Father of His Country*, Parts I, II, III and IV?"

"A rip-off of Flash's *Boss Tong of Hong Kong*, Parts I through VII," I sneered.

"My god! You know the Flash films of Francis Fong!"

I knew from the sudden beatific sheen on the man's baggy-eyed face that my life had turned an unexpected corner. Welcome to the Magic Kingdom. I kept my excitement low profile.

"A Fong homage," Ham Cohan explained, "not a rip-off." He stroked the same wrist he'd kissed, then gripped my hand and gave it a reverent shake. "I can't believe you know Fong's films! That makes you an automatic member of the Flash Fan Club. Want to know who else belongs? Tarantino and me."

Mimi crackled a message on Ham's walkie-talkie. "Arturo checked in. But dead drunk. He's a no-show for this afternoon."

"Gotta go," Ham apologized. But he was still beaming at me. "So you're a Fong fan. This has to be karma! Have lunch tomorrow? I'll send a car. Just stand at the corner there and Sam'll find you. Ciao until then!"

The first time I heard of karma was from the Indian burger-muncher at McDonald's, the one who'd asked me out to an Indian movie. A moonfaced man with heavy lids and a neat goatee, he'd made his move, then handled my rejection philosophically.

"Your no is not a personal disappointment," he'd lectured, "because it is evidently not in my karma to see you outside this eatery. So, what to do? Overdose on Sominex like my roommate, Mukesh, who was having brilliant career in biochemistry? No! The concept of karma is that fate is very dynamic. Not too many peoples are understanding that part of it. True concept of karma is: when on a dead-end street, jump into alternate paths."

I don't think Ham had that Indian man's concept of karma in mind when he sent his assistant for me. A woman was at the wheel of a blue Ford Escort. "I'm Sam," she called out to where I was squatting on the sidewalk next to Pammy and her pup, Whammy. "Samantha. Ham's assistant. He said you'd be expecting me."

The woman's face with its nose stud, tongue hoop and eyebrow rings didn't seem out of place at the corner of Cole and Haight. I tested her as a matter of principle. "How do you know you want me and not her? Or her? Or him?" It was a warm morning. Folks I didn't recognize from soup lines were staking out spots and propping up cardboard signs. GIVING FEELS GOOD, TRY IT! LOST MY TICKET HOME TO THE MOON, NEED HELP. Amateurs, transients. Trust fund derelicts. Dim prospects of futurity.

Samantha said, "The boss doesn't forget faces. He described you to a tee. Shall we?"

On the way to ShoeString Studios' offices in North Beach, in the middle of one of my harangues on the high-handedness of rich movie people who thought they could come into a neighborhood and treat us like dirt, she asked, "Wow! Did you feel that?"

"Feel what?"

"Three-point-two, at least. You know what I was doing when the last one hit? Weighing a Bulgarian in a Berkeley weight-loss clinic for nudists, and the man jumped naked off the scales and raced right out into Shattuck, that's a busy street!"

I hadn't felt any tremor. Probably because I wasn't tuned in to earthquake preparedness. I went back to haranguing.

Samantha didn't enjoy the drive as much as I did. When she showed me into Ham's office, I heard her whisper, "For your lunch, I recommend the Tums, boss."

Ham Cohan wasn't Asian according to Frankie's formula, but he was a man with more needs than wants. I sized him up before I'd clocked fifteen minutes in his office. He needed to wheel and deal in human vanities, needed to do favors so he would be owed, needed to break down doors for friends so he'd be admired and to rescue waifs like me so he'd be adored. I figure a guy who makes himself that indispensable must collect in imaginative ways. He didn't look it, but he could turn out to be more dangerous than Frankie.

At least Ham didn't come on direct, forthright, as Frankie had, which was just as well. I was off men for the while, smelling smoke, seeing flames, when I thought of sex. I was attracted to Ham. I don't deny it. It had to do with the game he played. Ham's game was devotion. Devotion tending to the melodramatic.

He sat me on a chair under a framed *The Father of His Country*, Parts I, II, III poster triptych while he networked for me on the phone. "Hi, Simone, what's up? Still desperate for a house sitter? . . . Does that mean what I think it means? . . . I think it means Padraic's out of the picture, et cetera. Well, mazel tov, darling . . . I'll ask around.

Shouldn't be impossible to find someone . . . I know, I know, you have psycho goldfish and nervous plants."

"I need a job, Ham. I have a place."

"Hi, Verna, how's the commute going? If you decide to spend the whole month with Larry in Tucson, I might be able to find you just the right tenant . . . Keep in touch, ciao!"

Pappy used to be a chain-smoker. Ham had to be a chain-telephoner.

"Hi, Jess, I have a very special friend sitting in my office . . . No, just arrived in town . . . Yeah, exactly, I'm trying to talk her into helping you out at the agency. Here, I'll put Devi on so you can work your charm on her . . . Just for a second, though, we're running late as it is . . . Day-Vee, yes . . . I don't think it's an Indian name, Jess. She hasn't mentioned anything about being named for any Indian village or mountain. You're thinking Uma, as in Thurman." He covered the mouthpiece. "Is it a Hindu name?"

I shrugged. "Got it off a license plate."

"Cool." He laughed.

I went with the laugh.

"Okay, see you at Glide Sunday? You bring whichever tight-ass author you're looking after this weekend, I'll bring my new friend. Ciao!"

"Who's Jess?" I asked.

"Just the woman who owns the hottest media escorting business in the country." He punched up another number.

"Why did your friend Jess think my name's Indian?"

Ham was still networking. "Hi, Francesca, *cara mia*, just checking in . . . Yeah, it's moving, the director hasn't shot himself in the head yet, and the cash cow from Osaka hasn't cut us off yet, so we aren't complaining . . . But how're *you* doing? . . . That's it, that's why I'm calling. I just met someone who'd be perfect for your restaurant. Jaqui may've beat you to it . . ."

Ham worked the phone, part agent, part producer and wanna-be lover; I paced his overfurnished office. After the sixth call I stopped eavesdropping and read aloud the names in fine print off Ham's posters of art films. *Lola Lavendar. Baby Tahbeez. F. A. Fong.* Frankie Fong high-kicking in *The Monster of Mandalay?* My Frankie in a pre-Flash horror flick? Guilt closed in. I let myself down into a chair directly below that poster.

"Weird," I remarked. I meant the Flash connection between us.

"He's moved to the States, you know." Ham put the phone down, and sighed. "It's sad, really sad. He's making videos for some exercise firm. The man was a genius."

Is, but I let the error pass.

"His house burned down in New York. Someplace up-state. I heard he's being investigated for murder and arson."

"Somebody died?"

"Some squeeze. Smoke inhalation."

I didn't have to believe the rumor about death from smoke inhalation. I didn't have to believe there was any fatality. I didn't have to believe there'd been a fire, except that I'd witnessed it.

"It must have been an accident. They said it was an old firetrap, and he'd added all sorts of electrical shit. Someone must have fallen asleep smoking. The cops picked him up 'cos he was screaming and running down the street like a maniac. The Oswald syndrome. He doesn't belong in a state pen! Jeez, the Flash was a genius."

I held my gaze on the Mandalay Monster. On the contrary, Flash was so vulnerable, a one-hundred-fourteen-pound woman destroyed him. *We knew that all along, bud, didn't we?*

Ham grinned, rolling his eyes up at the Mandalay Monster. "Acts like my ex-wife. Looks like all my ex-wives." He beat his chest in mock horror. "You see where romantics end up?"

"Where?"

"Living alone on houseboats. On the lam from exes, lawyers, creditors." He pointed to a Polaroid picture taped to the side of his computer. It was of an ordinary-looking houseboat, its name, *Last Chance*, painted in red across its prow. "It can be cozy." He gave me an it's-your-call kind of look. I must have scared him. "I'm starving, how about you? Wanna check out my favorite Chinese hole-in-the-wall?" He grabbed his jacket off a peg behind the door of his office and walked to the elevator while wriggling his arms into the sleeves. The jacket wasn't cut like the blazers and sports jackets men wore in Schenectady. It was loosely fitted and collarless. You had to be confident to wear that. What's next, sky-blue tuxedo with black piping?

Over lunch at Tung and Phuk on Stockton near Columbus, Ham went through a Coming-to-a-Theater-Near-You version of his life epic. Suburban childhood. Parochial schools. Dad into Knights of Columbus and the Irish Rovers, Mum into Jack Daniel's. Four surviving siblings, making adequate livings as photographer, graphics designer, prison warden and short-order cook. "I dropped out of Berkeley to look after Mum." He sang a bar from "Beauty School Dropout."

"Don't be so defensive," I soothed. I made the necessary entry in my mental Rolodex: Catholic; four divorces; no kids; impulsive but avoids commitment.

Ham turned his bad marriages into sitcoms, then prodded me. "Your turn, Day-Vee. I don't know a thing about you."

I chopsticked a perfect crisp-fried squid from its bed of spinach to Ham's lips. *Take your time,* I told myself, *craft a bio to charm, don't scare him with the little you know.*

"Give me your first impressions, Ham."

"Oh, streetwise in a way," he teased. "Actually, I see two people."

"Only two?" I teased back.

"I noticed the New York plates. You're about as Haight as a Japanese tourist." He squirted pepper sauce on his noodles. "You ever model, do a little acting? On the lam? Drugs, maybe?"

"Okay, you're good."

"New York's cool," he said. "New York's sexy."

I played to Ham's image of me. Mother was the innocent native-born Californian from one of those valley towns ending in *o*, a fun, normal late-sixties–early-seventies type who'd tried out all the good stuff like communes, bead curtains, Buddhism, drugs, headbands, drugs, lots of drugs,

Jimi, Janis, Morrison, am I missing something from those times, Ham?

Ham bought it, and played along. "Candlemakers on Telegraph, gurus on Sproul Plaza, ashrams in Napa. Jimi used to hide out in my place when he wanted to be with a chi—I mean, a woman—for longer than an hour. That's before all the booze and drugs, of course. Who knows, I might even have met your mother."

"Fucked her, you mean?"

Ham ignored that, and the distant implication. "That's the way it was. Where's she living now?"

"No clue."

"Tell me something new."

"She's dead, for all I know. Like Jimi and Janis."

"And if she isn't?"

She'll wish she were. But I didn't say that. I said instead, "I wouldn't know where to look. My legal parents— I was adopted when I was two—don't know and don't care to know."

Bio-Mom I painted as a flake who'd backpacked across three continents, chasing herbs and new gurus.

"Half the girls in Berkeley were on those trips." He got mawkish nostalgic, and looked like an old man all of a sudden. "The girls of our youth."

I stabbed at wilted greens that I didn't have names for. "Women," I corrected.

"Two of my wives knew their way around Katmandu a lot better than Oakland." He sighed. "And add to them, oh god! Laura Ann, Melanie, Loni, Jess, Cindi, the Holbrook twins . . ."

"I think my mother was different from the women of your youth."

Ham gave my knee a pat, then a squeeze. His message came through: the times had been unique, not the women. Your mother was the product of her times. I'm old enough to understand, to be your guide through it, not *that* old.

"Does my story bore you, Ham?" I said. "I can pitch it different. I should've known, you're a producer, not a friend."

"The war screwed us up." He wasn't speaking to me.

"I can think bankable script if that's all you want. Back-packing blonde and swarthy, mysterious guru meet cute."

I'd barely got started when Ham stopped me. "It's not that, hon, I'm not bored. No one's bored by the ocean. No one's bored by a tornado."

The Gray Nuns had named me Faustine after a typhoon, I remembered. Was my fury that obvious? "You find me scary, Ham?" I pulled my charmer pout. Frankie'd been putty when I pouted. "I scare you?" I waited for Ham to laugh. "Ham, what's wrong?"

"No force in nature stronger than a child trying to find her mother." He plucked a wad of bills from his inner pocket, peeled off a twenty without looking and called the waiter over.

"Everything satisfactory, Mr. Ham?" The waiter of-fered two fortune cookies; I grabbed one, Ham crushed the other and dropped the crumbs back on the tray.

"You're scary all right. You're trying to enlist me in a war, aren't you?"

It was true; I needed Ham, needed the nets he cast, the people he knew, the visions and delusions he'd survived. Without him I'd be drifting downstream in the trivia of my mother's times. I knew that their seventies had been more than cheap beads and headbands, but I was never easy about their music, never quite sure who'd died when of what self-indulgence. Forget their death-by-Nirvana and death-by-bombmaking; the truth was I had no experience of counterculture. In Wyatt's Circle in Schenectady, the most we could boast of was shoplifting or spray-painting. "Expressions of ad hoc spite against the Establishment" is how Wyatt dismissed our misdemeanors. I had to understand Ham and Bio-Mom and their Berkeley times. *The girls of Ham's youth.* That's when I made up my mind to let Ham seduce me. I could be the youth of Ham's middle age. Late middle age. Deep-fried squid is not the aphrodisiac.

He scraped his chair back across the red linoleum floor. "Poor fucking Jimi," he sighed. "Now you have me all depressed." He pulled the table forward so it'd be easier for me to slide out.

The cashier had the receipt and two more fortune cookies on a tiny plastic tray. "Everything fine?"

"Thanks, Lee." Ham picked one cookie off the tray and tossed it to me. "I never look."

I read my fortune. *Confucius says, Come back for marvelous meal to same restaurant.* Frankie would have been mortified; first we were sinister, now we're getting cute.

Ham took out a ballpoint and scribbled on the receipt. "Who do you want to be, hon? Staff? Talent? Consultant? In case the IRS wants to know."

"Force of nature," I said. Deal with that, Mr. Accountant. "In case the Flash ever asks."

The cashier said, "My grandson Byron, he has the acting bug, Mr. Ham."

We'd almost made it out the door.

"Why not send him over sometime? Who knows, maybe we'll cure him."

We walked out into lemony-gray afternoon brightness, holding hands.

In North Beach the afternoon was still warm, but the stretchy shadows thrown by commercial buildings got me down. I slipped my arm around Ham's waist as we strolled down a sloping block. "What now? What comes after squid?"

We were passing a café. A cozy café. Ham could have gone into it, ordered two espressos, we could have hunkered down at the wood counter and listened to Verdi.

Ham stopped. I caught his look. Sex, like grace, comes at you when you least expect it. "Your place?"

A mean question. "Not today," I said.

"My office then." We kept walking towards ShoeString. "You'll give me a VIP tour?"

"Maybe."

I was in the studio's guest suite on the floor directly above Ham's office. You needed a special key to a special elevator to get to it. That's where we found ourselves après-squid.

The whole floor was one big room, divided into purple and crimson alcoves for sleeping and partying. On the ceiling were murals of scenes from *The Father of His Country*, Part I. Fishing junks burning in a Hong Kong harbor. A half-naked white karate champ chopping bloody evil Japanese soldiers à la the young Frankie Fong. Grateful peasants stringing up fat tyrants. Asian belles with boob implants waving peacetime palm fronds.

"Like it?" Ham slid his hands under my T-shirt.

"A monument to yourself," I murmured, "must be the most satisfying kind." I let myself savor the probes and touches of those expert hands.

"Get you a drink?" The tip of Ham's tongue traced my hairline.

"I don't mind."

"Later," he whispered. The hands dragged themselves down my midriff. "Let's be indiscreet first."

I unbuckled Ham's belt, and tugged his shirttail out and over his pants, felt him harden. He let go of me to un-button his shirt. From just below the left collarbone to halfway down his chest, a scar cut diagonally through gray-brown chest hair. I kissed the scar. "I might tell you how I got it," he said, "when we have that drink." He stepped out of his slacks and shorts, but kept his socks and loafers on.

"Tell me how you like it," he coaxed, pulling me down on a sofa, and pushing me back against cushions. "It's all fair game." He knelt in front of me. "You taste sweet. Sweet and corrupt and tender and very young."

"Poor Ham," I whispered, "poor Jimi."

Afterwards we lay on the rug, and didn't talk about Ham's scar. We talked about safe things, like the perfect pet for a filmmaker (tropical fish), straight-to-video love affairs, dangerous women, what's left that's still sexy, still exciting.

"Got to go back to work sometime." He raised himself on an elbow. "Want that drink now?"

I reached under the sofa with my feet for my T-shirt. "I want a job now."

"That's easy." Ham pulled on his shorts. Gray-brown hair whorled above the wide waistband.

"Here's a harder one, then," I said to his back as he made his way to the refrigerator in the kitchen alcove.

"Want a Diet Coke?"

"I want a detective, Ham."

I called Ham's office from a pay phone near the Clayton Street post office the next morning. Between dreams the night before that I was sleeping in a bed and not a backseat, I developed an itch to drop Angie a postcard and tell her I was . . . well, I figured I'd come up with something if I bought a stamp and a postcard, but ended up dialing ShoeString.

"I'd have sent flowers," Ham said, "if I'd known where to send them."

"I don't have a vase for flowers, Ham."

"When can I see you again?" I heard him call out to his assistant, "Got that list, Sam?" Then he was back on the mouthpiece. "Got something to write with?"

I didn't, so I couldn't write down the four or five names of private investigators and agencies that he read off Samantha's list. The only agency names that sounded familiar were Vulture and Vulcan.

"So when?" Ham asked. "Don't I deserve a phone number at least?"

"I think we both like games," I said.

I got the Vulcan number from information—god! I hate paying for information just because all the phone books are chewed up or missing—and dialed it next. A woman's voice drowsy with decongestants instructed me to leave my name, number and the purpose of my call. I called the Vulture number. When the tape came on I introduced myself as "a very close friend of Ham Cohan." I didn't hang up right away, and sure enough, the same man who hadn't wanted to give me the time of day before said, "Okay, it's Fred Pointer."

"Ham Cohan thought you could help me."

"What did he say?"

"It's a missing-persons case—"

Fred cut me off. "What exactly did Ham say about me?"

I lied. "He said maybe you don't do missing persons anymore, but that you were the best. Let me just describe the case to you, Fred."

"Ham said that?"

"Yep."

"Ham doesn't like me. Why would he say that about me?"

"Because he admires you?"

"Ham knows I'm a persistent prick, I get things done."

"When's the soonest opening?"

"Middle of November. Of next year."

"How about today, Fred?"

"You're pretty persistent yourself." Fred laughed.

He gave me an early-evening slot for later that week, and suggested a coffee in my neighborhood.

"I'll come to your office. Easier that way."

"Name a coffee shop," he insisted. "What's your native habitat? I need to know the client."

"How about the Boss Bean?" I'd been inside only once; it looked like the kind of place that had survived many owners and many names.

"Start making notes," Fred counseled. "Whatever you have on the missing person, get it down."

"You mean, like tattoos and harelips?"

"Whatever the fuck you have. Anything. I figure if it's a harelip you don't need an expensive investigator like me."

Hint, hint, Mr. Pointer. Expensive is good. I can be First Class, too. I couldn't admit I didn't have a thing, not even a real name. "How'll you recognize me?"

"Relax, I'll find you." He hung up.

I called Ham again. "That drink you promised yesterday? What if I were to collect tonight?"

"How about right now?"

Tung and Phuk caters "Love Bird Specials" on houseboats of cash-paying special friends. We drove to Sausalito, listening to jazz tapes, stuff on his generation that I had to fake an interest in. Life is a learning curve for upstate orphans.

"Jazz at its best," he explained, "is all about white men acting black and black men acting white, for the sake of music."

Maybe because I wasn't one or the other, I never quite caught the difference between jazz and the blues or jazz and swing or, for that matter, jazz and anything that played on radio stations that advertised cruises, health care for seniors and IRAs. Ham's music just sounded old.

I wasn't tone deaf, like Pappy and Angie; I hadn't been *born* a DiMartino, thank god! I did know about twenty kinds of rock from my summer stint at the Record Barn in Latham Mall. Well, actually, I only knew all the songs and groups that'd made the charts in June and July 1992. But that expertise didn't count with Ham. Ham really hated rock—Whiteboy Noise, he called it—even more than he hated rap. Rock and rap, he instructed, were musically racist. I went along with his attitudes, because I liked Ham. And because I might need more favors. And anyway, what was not to like about Congo Master Poncho Sanchez when I wasn't having to pay nor wait in line?

Between tapes Ham disclosed surprise number two: I had a job cocktail waitressing two weeknights and weekends at Steep Steps, the jazz club to die for on Folsom.

I felt very special that afternoon. I thought at the time it was because I hadn't picknicked on Hot Peking Prawns before, hadn't been held and shaken on a boat, floating on floating, so insulated from the city and from time, hadn't ever made love through a quake big enough to knock cereal boxes off a galley shelf. Now I wonder if my feeling so special wasn't because Ham was scared of me, or maybe not of me but of what he'd started. He needed to believe I was some kind of fallen princess, not a no-name street person living out of a car and soup kitchens. He should've known I never belonged in that pool. But that afternoon on the *Last Chance* all those questions could be put aside. Squint your eyes just a little, and I looked like a boat-worthy, Sausalito-worthy, jazz-worthy Californian. A good life had been given us, and it would go on and on, and it would get better.

Ham told me the next morning—I'd scrounged together a breakfast of cranberry juice and Wheat Thins—that he'd called in his chips and found me a job in record time because he couldn't bear my sleeping in a car.

The Steep Steps job made it possible for me to move into a second-floor no-lease rental in a rooming house on Beulah Street off Cole. The house was a dilapidated Victorian with graffiti-tagged walls. CEE-DOUBLE-YOU, the kid got around. The stairs creaked; the hallways smelled of pot and the spices of the home of the brave. I was inching closer to the times, maybe even the block, of my flower-child Bio-Mom. I could only picture her as a teenager in batik and bell-bottoms. She existed outside time. I was already a lot older than she must have been.

My floor had an astrologer who read futures off a software called Disaster, a retired Belgian chocolatier and a Somali medical student who supported his wife and two kids, a bunch of sisters and an elderly woman by doing body piercing, body spackling, tattoo erasures and clitoridectomies. The ground floor had larger rooms and longer-term tenants, including a political refugee from a place he called Vanuatu (which I hadn't heard of before I met this huge, bitter man), a preschool teacher and her harpsichordist lover, a Serbian photographer with a name that was all consonants and behind a door hung with an I ♥ MY ARSENAL sign a Vietnam vet who painted made-to-order signs for a living. BLOWJOB BETTE'S B&B, COLE VALLEY MILITIA: you couldn't miss his work on Haight.

All my neighbors had come home to the Beulah rooming house from somewhere else. Vanuatu Man wasn't the only refugee, and Loco Larry wasn't the only war-maimed. Everything was flow, a spontaneous web without compartments. Somalia, Vanuatu, Vietnam, Belgium, India-Schenectady. Forty years ago it was a big one-family house, probably Italian. We shared toilets and kitchens. What counted was attitude. *Faithandhope.* I made that my daily mantra. Trust coincidence, aim for revenge. *Faithandhope.*

In this mood, I passed the collection bowl for Divine Intergalactica, xeroxed horoscopes and happiness charts for my astrologer neighbor, taught "Puff the Magic Dragon" to the small Somali boys and even let myself be waylaid on the stoop by Loco Larry, who picked up transmissions from morals squads and undercover agents. He could read their minds. He could smell entrapment, see purple glows around their fed heads. What was not to believe? Beulah belonged in a special-effects studio lot.

Three weeks into October, and I already could give guided tours of San Francisco's homeless and high rollers. Cocktail waitressing never felt like my vocation, but because the club was stuck between a pawn shop and a transsexuals' lingerie boutique, I acquired a wardrobe no DiMartino would recognize me in. On any given night Kiki, a recovering anorexic who shared my shifts, filled me in on which celebrity patron was nurturing what addiction, and Beth Hendon, the bartender as well as boss, when she was around, on who was fucking whom. The full dope on Beth I got from Ham. She had been a runway model in Paris, Milan, Buenos Aires, crashed in Miami, done the Betty Ford Center turnaround more than once and was currently trying out life as a small-business woman.

The Bay Area was good to me.

I intended to be good for it.

For meetings with strangers in public places like coffee shops, I like to wear a rose between my teeth. I talked Loco Larry the sign painter into providing me the rose for my preliminary checking out of the PI from Vulture. Larry was in a cooperative mood. My right cheek got a *quality* flower in fifteen different colors, the lips its calyx, the left cheek its thorny stem.

The Boss Bean is the kind of benign place where a salesman in shirt and tie doesn't stick out any more than a Schenectady runaway with a psychedelic rose on her face or a bag lady in sweats. You don't have to have shrapnel-studded brows or Mohawk hair. Nobody shoves around nobody else's aura. Everybody's made welcome to the Bay area. If you just hiked in from an aw-shucks county, the blackboard menu'll clue you in on cool, foreign pronunciations. Example: AU LAIT (*o-lay*) $1.50. The only other time I'd been inside this café had been with Archangel Gabe, and he'd walked out after I'd pointed to the menu and ordered the o-lay, muttering (much as Wyatt might have done, come to think of it), "And why not olé! Fuck the Haight, it's strictly for whitebreads!"

I pushed poor Wyatt out of guilt range, and ordered an olé and a bagel at the counter.

"Cool," the kid behind the counter said above the whoosh of steamed milk. "I like the way you say it. Makes for a fiesta in the head."

I carried my coffee and bagel to the row of tables by the wall-to-wall glass sliding door and took possession of the only table for two left overlooking Waller Street. Then I shifted my chair around and scanned faces for one that had "gumshoe" glowing in invisible ink on its forehead. None of the coffee-drinking males looked the right age. They still wore their baseball caps backwards, had too many rings in their lips and lobes. An HIV test came back positive on my right, and on my left a techie argument about too many Asians making the Internet boring. Two men in hard hats strode in for take-out lattes. Another seedy row house being gentrified, more Haight natives being expelled. An old man in winter coat, fur cap and galoshes loped in. He carried his own mug. It had a Yale logo. "How's it going, Lionel?" the kid behind the counter chatted as he filled the mug. "The Martians treating you any better today?"

A car honked on Waller, kept honking. A woman in a shapeless dress of expensive linen looked up, frowning, from her paperback. She was frowning at a yellow VW bug honking at a double-parked panel truck. The truck was Loco Larry's. The woman went back to reading *The Portable Chekhov.* She caught me staring, got up and grabbed a postcard advertising Tanqueray gin from a rack of freebie postcards and scribbled something on it. Then she popped the book into a canvas tote, gathered up her dirty glass, plate and fork and stacked them in a plastic bin that had a PLEASE! Magic-Markered on its side, stalked past my table, dropping the postcard on the floor near my feet, pushed the sliding glass aside and left the café. I didn't have to crane my neck to read her message: *Read "The Kiss" and Die.*

On Waller the driver of the VW bug had given up honking. I watched him sit on the sidewalk and do what looked like yoga breathing exercises.

A tall, bald man came in, wheeling a bike. He had the shaved legs of a competitive bicyclist. He didn't go to the counter and order an herbal tea as I'd expected. He came straight to my table. "No fun when you make it easy." He grinned at the rose on my face. "Fred," he said, "Fred Pointer. Let's get started." The grin didn't lighten up the harrowed blue of his eyes.

"Get you a tea?"

"How about we walk around some and you fill me in. I'm not saying yes yet. As Ham told you, I don't take missing-persons cases."

"It's a mission, not a case," I shot back.

He gave me a strange look. "Maybe you need a shrink more than you need me."

"Ready?" I left my dirty dishes on the table, and led the man from Vulture out of the café.

We walked; I talked. Of Mama and Pappy, of Celia, of Wyatt, of Mr. Bullock and his silly assignments. I kept talking. I couldn't stop talking. It became as easy as breathing. I described the smell of lye in an outhouse, the furry touch of spiders crawling over my legs, the pooling of sap-white blood of roaches I swatted dead, I tasted stony grit in orphanage gruel, I felt panic as fingers closed around my throat. I hadn't remembered any of it, not until that moment. We kept walking. Away from the Haight.

Fred Pointer dug fast and dug deep. He called me back in less than a week. "What I have isn't necessarily pretty."

I arranged for him to meet me at Steep Steps as I came off my Friday-night–Saturday-morning shift. "Want to call off the dogs?" And when I didn't say yes or no, he added, "No guarantees except that it'll be expensive."

I said I wanted to know what he knew before I decided whether to stay in or quit.

We went in our separate cars to an all-night diner in the Tenderloin. There was only one other patron, a slick fifty-something Eurasian man in leather pants and Elvis hair on a stool at the counter. The man was sipping water out of a highball glass. It may have been gin or vodka in the glass. A khaki duffel bag and cheap vinyl carry-on were on the floor by his booted feet. He was chatting up the waiter, probably Vietnamese, in some Asian language and making the stool seat spin half turns. The waiter kept his head down and wet-mopped around the bags.

Fred picked his way to the table farthest from the counter. "Can we get some service?"

The waiter looked up but didn't stop mopping. "Yeah?" he said.

Fred Pointer ordered hot water and a slice of lemon. "What'll you have?" he asked me. "You're paying."

I ordered a Coke. "So lay the good news/bad news on me," I begged.

"Pepsi," the waiter said.

"Okay, Pepsi."

Fred said, "You're pretty special, Devi."

"I knew that," I snapped.

The waiter propped the handle of the wet mop against the table next to ours, and went off for the Pepsi.

"No, I mean different special."

"How different?"

"Two continents went into your making. That means you're one up on Kurtz, Devi."

Kurtz was probably a mixed-race local rock star. I'd ask Ham to get me a freebie to a Kurtz concert. "Well, not that special," I countered. "There's the late Klaus Nomi, and—"

Fred said, "Shut up, okay. Let me do the talking."

"Go ahead," I pouted.

"I've exchanged a couple of faxes with a fellow in Bombay. I worked on a case with this fellow must have been five years ago. He didn't recognize the name you gave, but he said he remembered there'd been juicy stuff in all the papers about a sex-guru serial killer and his harem of white hippies, he thought way back in the seventies. He's checking it out."

"How do you know this man's reliable? Have you met him?"

"Who? Rajeev Raj? He'd kill if he had to. When we had him work on the case I mentioned, it was the usual post-custody-hearing kidnapping thing, he tracked the kid and his dad down to a beachfront hotel in Goa, broke into the room, beat up the dad and kidnapped back the kid. He's efficient."

"So what're you saying? There's a possibility that my mother was in that harem?"

"The years fit. The region fits. Who knows, maybe you have half brothers and sisters roaming the world. He's supposed to have fucked all the members of his happy hippie family. A lot of those gals didn't make it back. White slave traffic, Saudi sheikhs, jaundice, cholera, want me to go on?"

"My mother came back to California." Pappy'd paid her airfare back, but I didn't get into the money angle.

"You don't know it was your mother, do you? That's why I say, it could get expensive."

"Males too?"

"He'd fuck a cockroach if it were big enough, that's his rep. What we used to call polymorphous perverse."

Fred made that phrase sound a fun type to be. Even if I owed my existence to two of those sex-cult bozos, I didn't have to out-polymorphous-perverse them; in fact I didn't have to believe Fred and his Mr. Raj. "How do I know you aren't kidding?"

"What do you want from me, jokes?" He parted his lips slightly, and moved his lower jaw laterally a couple of times. "Hear it pop?" he asked. "It's tensing up. I could use some jokes myself. You know, loosen up."

"What else did your man in Bombay fax?"

"What's that supposed to mean?" He pummeled lemon pulp with the back of his teaspoon. "That you want me to give the green light to Rajeev? He won't come cheap."

What choice does an orphan have? Ignorance is no choice.

"You want to sleep on it, and call me tomorrow?"

"Get me what you can find, Fred."

"I'll get you what there is to be found, period." He stood, a tall man with a tortured face. The top of his bald head glowed in the diner's silver-blue light. That's the way a fed's head must look to Loco Larry. "I'm the goddamn best there is." He checked his watch. "What you do with the stuff, I don't need to know. Goodnight."

"What time's it in Bombay?" I asked Fred's long-waisted back.

"Thirteen and a half hours into tomorrow. Goodnight."

Leatherpants on the bar stool said something that sounded dirty. He was looking at me, but speaking in loud Vietnamese to the waiter, who'd vanished into a storeroom for my cola. Putting together the two and two of my drama with Fred and getting it wrong, I assumed.

I took two dollar bills out of my wallet for Fred's hot water with lemon wedge, but didn't leave the diner with him.

The waiter came back with my Pepsi in a glass.

"I've changed my mind," I said.

"You can't change your mind now," the waiter said. "Too late. You ordered a Pepsi. I brought you a Pepsi. Drink or no drink it, that's your problem."

I started to walk out of the waiter's arm range. The waiter made a halfhearted show of blocking my path with his mop. Leatherpants slid off the stool and gave his duffel bag a quick, vicious kick. The duffel caught me in the left ankle before I could get to the door. My ankle felt as if it'd been clubbed, but I wasn't about to give Leatherpants the satisfaction of a howl or yelp. I stepped over the duffel bag, and hissed, "The INS is on its way, mister."

The man on the stool hooted. "And fuck you too, doll!"

"Hey!" I heard the waiter's voice behind me. "Hey, you owe for Pepsi!" But he chose not to chase me. The wet mop was still going swish-swish and the man on the stool was still laughing when I left the diner.

The other day a man driving home from work on I-80 was shot by a sniper near Davis. The man usually stopped for a beer, but that day his son was pitching Little League, and nothing, he'd promised, would keep him away. He was the third red Honda Civic with bumper stickers to pass under the bridge between five and five twenty-five, fulfilling all five preconditions set by his anonymous executioner for moral target practice.

The other night in Oakland, the proud owner of an Asian-run market closed early for his daughter's wedding. While celebratory firecrackers were being set off in Orinda, an elderly neighborhood woman was knocking on the store's shuttered door looking for her usual small bag of scented kitty litter. The woman could have waited—the cat didn't care—but she loved her cat Melba, named after an aunt, and so she embarked on a trek to the supermarket three long blocks away. She stepped off the curb without looking and was run over by a thirteen-year-old who'd stolen the car from in front of a 7-Eleven where the car's owner was counting out enough change to pay for a Snickers bar and a quart of skim milk.

The other week a refugee, just arrived in San Jose from Banja Luka by way of camps and detention centers, was stepping out of the third-floor offices of a relief organization with his care package of groceries, old clothes and used blankets when a shoot-out erupted between two just-formed girl gangs, the Pretenders and the Prissies, in the hallway, and a shot from a .30-gauge Chinese-made pistol ricocheted off the elevator into his skull.

The other month two high school dropouts from Stockton, hired for three grand by a cheated-upon wife to do a beat-to-a-pulp job on her pharmacist husband, were driving north on I-5 towards the drugstore when a highway patrolman stopped them for seat-belt and open-container violations. The pharmacist's still dispensing pills and trying to work things out with his wife.

We don't paint the lines on our palms, says Madame Kezarina aka Linda Szymborska-Wakamatsu. My take is different. Convergence is coincidence.

A daughter bumps into her runaway mother, what coincidence could be more natural?

All the same, I call Fred Pointer at his office. He's out of town, his tape tells the caller, but the caller may leave a brief message. "Give it to me fast, Fred," I whisper into the tape, "and fuck the cost!"

I first encountered Ham's old flame Jess in an upscale clothing store on Fillmore near Sacramento. Ham and I'd taken in a matinee at the Clay, and were ambling south towards Japantown for a bowl of *soba*. By then we'd slept together—"pleasured each other" was his phrase—a total of seven times.

If Ham's beat-up Triumph hadn't been in the garage, if I hadn't been leery of riding a bus or taxi that afternoon, neither of us would have thought of dashing into Dahlia's Divan and trying on pricey silk caftans and harem pants and making nice to the designer, Dahlia Metz, who happened to be one of Ham's many exes. Keeping the history of Ham's bawdy relationships straight was tough. Dahlia struck me as a wider-bodied Roseanne in stretch-velvet tunic and pants. She'd discovered her talent, she explained, in a women's prison in Afghanistan way back when everyone who was anyone put in time in Turkish or Afghan prisons. I wasn't sure if Dahlia's talent-discovery experience had come before or after her marriage with Ham. She pulled a layered dress off a rack, and held it against my chest. "Perfect," she said to Ham's mirrored reflection. "I call it the Seven Veils Dance, so watch out, Ham!"

I grabbed the wispy end of the outermost layer, and

twisted it around a forearm. *"Bodacious bodywear for audacious amateurs . . ."* I caught myself before I'd said, And Frankie, now your turn!

Dahlia experimented on me the many ways of wrapping or draping the Seven Veils dress.

Ham came through. He didn't have quite the Fong flair, but for a novice he wasn't at all bad. He said, *"After debauched days and delectable nights, the veiled Virgin of Varanasi whipped out a scimitar and whacked off the ponytailed pate of the perpetrator."*

"The maharani," I shouted, *"and the maidservant make out on a mustard-hued mattress while pesky pachyderms pirouette . . ."*

"Meanwhile the cuckolded codger carries his carbine and takes cracks at crocodiles and cranes, and his cantankerous councillors commit . . . What do they commit, for chrissake?"

". . . commit calumny with calamitous consequences," I finished for Ham.

Dahlia pulled the wispiest layer over my head and let it cover my nose and chin.

"Hold it!" Ham shouted at Dahlia. "Do it again!"

"What, Ham?"

"Does she remind you of Hedy Lamarr or what?"

He crooked his fingers, making a perfect box, and framed my face. Like Frankie, he was seeing possibilities in me at the most inappropriate, passionate moments. I tried to rescue the Fong word game. *"Heedful Hedy hides her head in a hole hollowed out of . . ."*

That's when a hard-bodied, graying blonde in a tight

silk T-shirt and linen shorts barged in on us from behind a rack of caftans. "Let me guess, Ham! A long-lost daughter come to collect support money?" Then she hooked her elbow around Ham's neck, and dragged his face close enough to hers to kiss. Ham did. Long and hard. I didn't check for tongue positions before announcing, "Hi, I'm Devi. Ham's friend."

Ham flinched, then let go his hold. The woman didn't step away from him. I took Ham's arm in an undaughterly way. The woman flicked blond bangs off her sun-aged face and, smiling, seized Ham's free arm. "Aren't you going to introduce an old flame to Devi?" she said.

I knew not to let her snideness rile me, but I did envy her overmuscled biceps and self-confidence.

Ham introduced the woman as Jess DuPree, the Jess of media escort agency Leave It to Me, didn't I remember him calling her that first time I stopped by his office? Wasn't she the one who always came through for him?

"ME," Jess said. "Media Escort, get the pun?" She gestured towards the fitting room. "Benita Farias, the mystery writer. Needs a softer look. TV's cruel."

I didn't need Madame K's computerized crystal ball to figure out that Jess and Ham had had—probably still had—a heavy thing going. For a fiftyish woman, Jess could still turn heads. She dismissed me as the newest on Ham's arm. I knew that because she said to Ham, "I think you're ready for a red Miata."

Over *soba* and fishcakes in Japantown I got the Jess & Ham Story, Abbreviated Edition. Yes, they'd been lovers in Berkeley. They'd co-protested McNamara's Vietnam, they'd co-organized a takeover of Sproul Hall, they'd co-lobbed rotting fruit at a motorcade that should have been escorting President YankeeStooge NguyenSlime, and for a while they'd cohabited in a commune. The commune living on Derby Street must have been as far back as in the fall of 1967, because by the spring of 1968 they'd moved on to Napa and coworshiped at Baba Lalji's feet.

Baba Lalji?

Oh, he was a guru guy who set himself up in an ashram before going on to bigger things.

Like what, Ham? Like sex, drugs and prison time?

No, more like gunrunning and Cold War politics. Ham filled me in on Hesse and Hinduism and Holymen with funny names like God-ji and Rishi-ji who came over on tourist visas and when the visas expired founded ashrams.

Ashram?

Ham could have made a living as a teacher or a preacher. He was most inspired when he was explaining. "Devi," he said, "think of Baba Lalji's Napa ashram as a B and B in wine country. Pure air, great meditating, tantric fucking, holistic healing, the works, and all of it gratis!" He said he'd lost track of Jess after her abortion.

"Love and abortion in a Napa B and B?"

Ham ignored the dig. "Think Vietnam, Devi. Think big Uncle Sam fucking over bandy-legged little VCs. Think McNamara fucking over bennied-out grunts. Rent the *Apocalypse Now* video if you can't think. You made your life one continuous flying fuck or you didn't survive the times."

"Jess had an abortion?" I was thinking, in spite of everything, I was glad Bio-Mom hadn't.

Ham changed the subject. "You're a cheap date," he said. "That must be why I've fallen for you. The one woman who keeps me solvent." He pulled a fistful of crumpled twenties out of a pants pocket and paid for our fishcakes and noodles with two bills and waited for change. "Got to be back at ShoeString right away, a call's coming in from Bangkok," he said. "I'll give you a ride home."

"I'm not going home." That part was true. "I'm meeting a friend."

"I'll drop you where you need to be. No trouble."

"I don't mind taking MUNI."

"If you don't want the person you're meeting to run into me, say so." He grabbed my wrist, and twisted it, but not hard enough to hurt. "Be straight with me, hon. Otherwise there's no relationship."

Relationship sounded so dated. "It's nobody you'd be interested in, Ham."

"Let me be the judge."

"It's nobody you'd want to meet. This guy's weird, really weird. He lives in my building. Loco Larry." My plan was to barge into the Vulture office and check out the latest fax.

"Loco as in 'crazy'?"

"Hates immigrants, hates feds. Hangs an I 'HEART' MY ARSENAL on his door."

"Is that the guy in army surplus on your stoop?"

"Not surplus. He's shown off knife slits and old blood."

"Poor fucker! Guys like him had their brains fried."

"Was it your baby? Did you love Jess, Ham?"

"What baby?"

"The abortion. You said something about an abortion . . ." Abortion, abandonment, adoption: all options in Bio-Mom's era had begun with the letter *a*.

The waitress came back with Ham's change, but didn't stick around for the tip.

"You mean the fetus?" He made expense account notes on the back of the receipt. "I'm no chauvinist, that's too easy. You can't be that lazy."

Embarrassed, I backed off. "I didn't mean it that way."

I showed my gratitude by asking for a new favor. Ham liked being asked, so we were trading favors. "Get me together with Jess? It'll bring me one step closer to your Berkeley times."

"Just be yourself and she'll come to you," he said. But he looked pleased. "How's Thursday night? Vito's, after nine." He made a note of it on the restaurant receipt.

Getting into clubs like Vito's was a breeze if you had Ham. Hanging with him meant your life was in the commuter lane, no waiting, no hang-ups, zipping right along while taxpayers sat fuming. Clubs were free; movies were seen months before release; musicians worked his name into songs. Everybody owed him. He needed to be owed. He was lonely. The loneliest is the person with the largest entourage.

I joined the debtors. That's as far as I could go in the commitment business.

"I'm not saying you aren't special, Devi," Linda, my psychic neighbor, warned. "But so's everyone. Take anyone in our building, take anyone in the universe. You think that poor schmuck from that Van-whatever place isn't special when there's a bounty on his head? And how about the little girls who traipse up our stairs to get their cunts sewn by the resident charlatan? Let me tell you about a client I'm counseling."

We were sharing oven space. I was heating up the last slice of a soy-cheese, artichoke and clam pizza, and Linda was roasting herbs guaranteed to lower blood pressure. Loco Larry was in our upstairs kitchen too, defrosting the fridge with a mallet and a spatula, but he had on his Walkman. Like the blonde with the DEVI vanities at the state line, Larry knew to make himself the center of the world that mattered.

"Just a normal kid," Linda went on. "Pacific Heights. Nice parents, nice siblings, decent grades. But in his previous life he was an Indian from India. The kid threw bombs, shot up cops, gave the British Raj a tough time. Such a hard time that the British shipped him off to a convict island and hanged him. Last winter the family finally took a trip to this island. The Andamans? Heard of it? It's a tourist trap now. Lots of fat Germans with fancy cameras checking out the empty prisons. But here's the thing. This kid from Pacific Heights found the spot on the wall of his old jail cell where he'd scratched his name with his fingernails. The kid leads his folks straight to the wall and reads off his name as though Indian's his mother tongue!"

I accepted Linda's chastisement. Every life is special. Some wondrous events transpire without making tabloid headlines. Linda was born in a displaced-persons camp in Germany, spoke her first word (*cuidado!*) in Argentina, married a Japanese doctor in Brazil and divorced him in Chile, then found fulfillment as a psychic in the Haight.

So here's my not-so-special history as Fred Pointer told me in installments during early-morning runs at the Golden Gate Park.

In a small-town courthouse in Rajasthan, India, Mr. Raj, the Bombay associate of Vulture, located files of cases going back further than fifty years. The files were bundled into bedsheets and cloth squares by year and month by court clerks and stacked on tops of cabinets by sweepers. Mr. Raj has also heard Hari, the oldest resident of Devi-gaon, a village now in danger of being swallowed by the town with the courthouse, tell lurid tales of a sahib and his memsahibs who smoked hemp, danced naked and made human sacrifice.

Hari, half blind and long retired as watchman of the courthouse, won't give up his broken stool to younger gatekeepers who can read and write but who can't remember as far back as Hari can.

Here's a transcript of one of three conversations Mr. Raj had with Hari, though something may have been lost or doctored in Mr. Raj's translation.

> *This happened some time ago, I was working as chief chowkidar in tourist bungalow where rich ladies from foreign came for spotting birds in every bush, shrub and tree.*
> How many years ago, Hari? Ten years, twenty years?
> *I answer your question with my own question. I ask you, sir, I ask you who wear expensive watch bought in foreign, what is time when our universes rise many times and fall many more times within one eye-wink of God Brahma? When this event came to pass, I was a fit fellow, I was carrying three–four suitcases on my head and running from the train station to the tourist guest house with no stop, no drop, no cough. No arthritis in neck nor knees, and my teeth . . . my teeth were so strong I used to chew sugarcane stalks . . .*
> So what was the crime you witnessed, Hari? What did the foreigners do?
> *The sahib and memsahibs? The ones who danced naked before they sacrificed one mem and one baby?*

Here Mr. Raj resorts to summary. It was a cold night, because Hari was wearing a wool vest, a scarf and what the PI identifies as a "monkey cap" with slits for eyes and lips. Hari and three cronies were drinking country liquor in a dead rajah's palace ruins when the sahib drove into view in a huge, fancy automobile. The sahib looked like a Bombay film "hero," only more handsome. Hari described him as wearing blue jeans like Bombay film stars, and moving the way a cheetah springs for the kill.

Then it's back to transcript format.

Hari, did you witness the killings?

I am saying a killer's hands began a job. Whether the hands were guided by the killer's head or by the killer's fate, who can say?

But you admit that you were present at the scene. Is that correct, Hari?

I was present and also not-present. How can we attain Nirvana if we say this is this and only this and that other is that other and only that other when this is a guise of that and when these are those and these-those are one single undifferentiated thing? I will say this much, sir, I was smoking bidi with my friends and we were drinking home-brewed toddy in palace ruins and the sahib and his two memsahib were visible smoking hemp and drinking bottled whiskey.

So what was the MO? Hari, how did the sahib do his killing?

First everybody was living. One, two, three and the baby, so altogether four dancing and singing. Then two became corpses and two kept dancing.

Then you reported the incident to the police.

You think I'm a fool, sir? You think police wouldn't lock me up as low-caste chowkidar with toddy on his breath and accuse me of the killing and stealing?

Did you not report the murders?

I ran fast-fast to sore grease women. Sore grease are old women from foreign but they have been in Devigaon so long they no longer act like memsahib. I told the sore grease women about the dead baby and the dead memsahib.

[N.B. "Sore grease" caused me some extra time, for which I shall not bill your client. I consider it personal research. The phrase means "Gray Sisters," but in French, bounced back to local English. "Sore grease"'s original spelling may be "Soeurs Grises."]

admired, then kept killing to be noticed. I was back in Frankie Fong's Asia: *hot, smoky, full of liars and cheats.* In Bio-Dad's overcrowded Asia, how does even an ambitious killer get himself noticed? No media coverage, no computerized Victim-Net, no milk cartons, no xeroxed flyers.

In Bangkok the lovers quarreled. They made up in Bali, to break up again in Surabaja. In Katmandu he added a Romanian to his harem. In Colombo, a Swiss. In Kabul he spent a day in jail for cursing a policeman. In all these cities, and in Chiang Mai, Srinagar and Taipei, he strangled, he conned, he made love to women he liked and to women he scorned and, who knows, maybe left my half siblings behind. In Singapore the lovers quarreled one final time. The woman went to the Singapore police and ratted on the man. She accused him of having strangled give or take seventeen men and women. The cops locked her up on drug-peddling charges, and passed her stories on to Interpol. Two Interpol agents interviewed her, and one of them believed her. She repeated her story about the seventeen murders, and went into detail about the when, where and how they'd been committed. She said nothing about the two killings in Devigaon, *she said nothing about me at all.* Interpol tracked her lover through Turkey, Thailand, Indonesia, Sri Lanka, to a hill station in India. The name the lover gave the Indian police when they booked him was Romeo Hawk. The suspect confessed to killing five, but was convicted of killing nine and sentenced to nine consecutive life sentences. He let Mr. Raj visit him in jail on condition that Mr. Raj brought him the latest Tom Clancy and a carton of cigarettes.

"Rajeev says the guy's a nutrition purist and a work-outaholic. The cigarettes were for bribing guards," Fred explained.

Rajeev Raj has met Bio-Dad; I envy him that. I don't have any idea what he looks like and what he sounds like. Smooth as butter, I'll bet. I got my good looks from him, and my fantastic good luck. So I chant Frankie's Asia mantra. *Hot, smoky, full of liars and cheats and murderers.* But all I can picture is a pair of hands. The hands swat at flies, scorpions, spiders, roaches. The cell floor is thick with bug corpses.

I didn't have to go on those dawn walks in Land's End with Fred. I didn't have to authorize Mr. Raj's trip to the shabby retreat house of Les Soeurs Grises in Mount Abu. I didn't have to find out what act of charity Sister Madeleine Corveau, originally of Lévis, Quebec, had performed in Devigaon the same night that Hari'd come running to her with his tales of human folly and wickedness.

Sister Madeleine spoke to Mr. Raj in the Devigaon dialect. She'd lived in the village for over forty years. Mr. Raj translated and summarized what he thought important. Fred hadn't brought the full report with him. Too bulky, he claimed. He pulled a couple of sheets out of his sweatpants and handed them over.

"She was near death," Mr. Raj reported Sister Madeleine's having said.

> *Minutes from death. I saw her, but not right away. It was a dark night, and I had only my torch. I'd missed her at first because she had crawled under the poor woman's*

*skirt, the dead woman's, may her soul rest in peace. Only
when I tried to lift the dead, the dead are so heavy,
no? . . . it was horrible, too horrible. Fortunately we kept
all kinds of anti-toxins in our little dispensary. Villagers
get snakebites, liquor poisoning, rabies. They come to the
Soeurs Grises. The sore grease, they call us. Some stay
around and find Jesus. Not anymore, you understand.
People don't want us here anymore, the country doesn't
want foreign missionaries. Now I'm a pariah. But I don't
remember French, I can't dream of Lévis.*

I take it that you saved the child, Sister?

Jesus did.

Afterwards you arranged the adoption? I know your
order places children in Europe, America and Canada.

*We did the only right thing under the circumstances. We
took the child to her mother.*

But the mother was in jail, wasn't she?

*Ministering to women prisoners, especially firangi [for-
eign, white] women prisoners, that was one of our duties.
The warden told us the mother wanted cigarettes. So first
time, we came with a Bible and two packs of cigarettes.
Next time we came with Faustine, and more cigarettes.
That was the name we gave, we named our orphans like
typhoons, Adele, Bella, Catherine . . . she was our sixth
that year, such a pretty little imp.*

The prisoner must have been overjoyed, Sister.

*The damned construe the Good Lord's interventions as
curses. The woman thanked us for the cigarettes.*

I dealt with that sucker punch by handing the sheets
back to Fred. The sun floated out over the bay, like a
balloon.

"I should be heading back," Fred said. "I do have other
clients. I have a life, you know."

"Who's stopping you?" I stalked off ahead of Fred. He
didn't follow.

The trail felt steep, stark, damp. A man on a mountain bike passed me slowly. Then he wheelied around. He cut two tight loops around me. He watched me, but said nothing. He had on a camouflage jacket. He hadn't been in any wars; he'd fried his own brains. I felt sad for Loco Larry. I felt sad for the baby girl the Gray Nuns'd brought to visit the prisoner. I felt sad for all the dumped and discarded. I heard the cypresses wail.

As Ham scouted free parking not too far from Vito's, I slipped in my question. "About Jess and you . . ."

They'd been involved. At one time or another he'd been involved, he said, with all the women I had met, or might meet, through him. "Serially," he added. "I'm not a lech, if that's what worries you."

"That's all you'll say?"

He slowed down. A man in a Lexus had either just pulled into a metered spot or was getting ready to pull out. The overhead light was still on.

"That's it?"

Ham tapped the steering wheel. "Don't believe everything you hear."

"It's just the body count that makes me wonder," I said.

Lexus Man stepped out his car with a fat smile on his thin face. I thought: *If I had a gun, I'd kill you. You don't know how close you came.*

Ham moved forward, still prowling for space. "You were never there, hon. It happened once in my lifetime. It was over quickly and it never came back." He grabbed my shoulder with his free hand.

From the way his face looked, I thought he was going ballistic on me. But when he finally spoke, his voice was melancholic. "We're the fucking freaks now. We're the surviving core, that's what you'll be looking at tonight." He slackened his grip, and I eased my body closer to the passenger-side door. "We created the Age, and we created the Scene. We created all of it, flower power, acid, free speech, rock, protest . . . Leary and Kesey and Brautigan, they got it from us."

I got the gist. All of them should have died thirty years before. They had friends who had, others who'd changed their lives and moved into the Establishment. Like Jess, like Ham, like Fred. Even old Bio-Mommy.

"We're just like the Nam vets." Ham sighed. "A lot of casualties, even more fucked-up survivors. And quite a few traitors." He brightened. "We came closer to destroying this nation than any group at any time in history. And we end up the Rodney Dangerfield generation."

He pulled into a parking lot and prepaid the attendant. We walked into Vito's in that odd, ambivalent mood.

Inside the club the lights were kept so low that it took me a few minutes to make out faces. He slow-guided me around crowded tables. People caught his eye and shouted his name. We stopped and chatted. "Aren't you going to introduce her, Ham?" some of them kidded. "At your own risk," Ham kidded back. "My friend Devi."

Vito's had a small dance floor packed with serious dancers, mostly Cuban. Ham was big on salsa music. My SUNY marketing degree didn't come in handy for telling mambo from bolero from tango from samba from salsa, and doing the macarena didn't count with Ham.

Given my guide, everyone assumed I belonged. They also assumed I'd come to California from somewhere more fascinating. All of a sudden Brazilians led off speaking to me in Portuguese, Zydecos in Creole, Mexicans in Spanish. The whole world had gone into my making, wasn't that Fred's complaint? The whole world was mine to claim. I shut my eyes for a moment as I floated through the club on Ham's arm. If I squeezed my eyelids harder, kept squeezing, I was sure I'd start speaking the language I'd shared with Sister Madeleine.

"You okay?" Ham whispered. "We won't stay long."

His lonely-man entourage swelled as we made our way to the booth that Jess DuPree was holding. She waved, all biceps, no flab. Her friends waved. Fred Pointer looked up, didn't wave. Of course he'd know Jess; everyone was in the loop except me. Fred acted as though we were meeting for the first time, a good PI trick. The game seemed harmless, so I played along. We spilled into adjoining booths, took over and joined tables. Ham reigned, king of lounge lizards.

Ham's groupies were mostly single-again thirtysomethings. Only two of his women friends—Jess and a bony hat-wearer with two nose rings—were the right age to interest me. The Hat-Wearer shot me bitter, brooding looks, but didn't speak to me. She wasn't speaking to anyone. The only communicating she did was to press up real close to Ham and tap his arm whenever she wanted another drink.

I answered the routine questions. Ham worked the booth. "How do you like our Bay Area?" "Do you kids still come to the Haight?" "Has someone taken you wine tasting through Napa?" I kept my deflectors up. "Gee, I don't know!" "Oh, wine goes to my head!"

Jess busted the routine with her "Devi, where are you from?"

"Upstate New York."

"I mean, where are you really from?"

I knew, but played dumb. "From Schenectady. Up near Albany."

"You know what I really mean, Devi. Come on, where are you from?"

"Some toxic dump. I'm a radioactive geek, can't you tell."

Ham stopped our sparring. "That's how I'd describe Schenectady too. Anyone aching to salsa?"

"Vámonos!" Jess laughed. She plucked the Hat-Wearer's hand off Ham's arm, and led him away.

I caught Fred's wince as Jess and Ham hit the dance floor.

Until I watched Jess move on that tiny floor, I hadn't figured salsa for a courtship dance. Retreat and pursuit. Promise and withhold. All longing and heartache. Ecstasy without messy consummation. Jess should be my double, not my rival.

"Life's a bitch," Fred muttered beside me, "and I know her." He signaled a waitress.

He must have had something going with Jess. I felt sorrier for the waitress. Satin shorts and a halter top, and probably two kids eating cold pizza at home. Life's a bastard, too.

Fred ordered rum. He didn't ask me what I might want. "An investigator is put on this earth to dig up dirt, right?

It's in his genes. Everybody's got something hidden. I lift the rock. It's a mission. You know about missions, Devi. Everyfuckingbody has slime tucked away."

I didn't hear Jess walk up behind me until she stuck a finger between my shoulder blades. "I'm really very boring," she said. It sounded like a warning.

"We weren't talking about you," said Fred. He reached for her hand and got fingertips. "Wanna give me a chance?"

"And have you find all those bodies? No thanks." Jess slipped out of Fred's range. We watched her head back to the dance floor. The way she moved she had to know we were watching. Ham was on the outer edges, sweating out a salsa number with a Latina in pink knit. She cut in on Pink Knit.

There are moments when I can't tell the difference between lunacy and luminosity. The Creator passes off riddles as meanings. Invisible weights pin me. One of those moments came on as I watched Fred watching Ham and Jess hugging. Crisscrossing destinies. I was part of the tableau, but I didn't know how or why.

"Let it go, Fred," I pleaded.

"Shit!"

"The center's a zero, Fred. Work the peripheries."

The Hat-Wearer suddenly came out of her coma. "Whoa, that's deep, that's so otherworldly. Did you just get back from Dharmasala?"

I risked a laugh. It came out hoarse, mean. "Not in this life," I mumbled.

The Hat-Wearer concentrated her stare on my chin. Her eyes were so pale they seemed flesh colored. "The universe is doughnut shaped," she said.

"That's good," Fred snapped. "So why not write fortunes for fortune cookies?"

I felt the pressure of Fred's palm on my thigh. I glanced up, but his sad eyes were on Jess and Ham on the dance floor. Remake of the Frankie/Ovidia/Debby Triangle, starring middle-aged whitebread. Debby'd burned Frankie's house down, and possibly killed a rival. Devi was more mature, but you wouldn't dis her and get away with it.

Fred played his misery low-key. "Say goodnight for us to everybody," he told the Hat-Wearer. "I'm driving Devi home." I let him hustle me out of the booth. Nothing wrong with some private time with Fred. A bonus, in fact. "Ciao!" I said.

Somewhere on Geary, Fred said out of the blue, "She tried to leap off the bridge, I know."

"Who? The weirdo in the hat?" But I knew he was talking about Jess.

"She tried to kill herself."

"She looks so . . ."

"Teflon?"

"So . . . so buff, Fred."

"Her second try."

"A long time ago?"

"Not long enough."

I kept my finger on the release button of the seat belt, chin angled down. "Looks like we've both been abandoned, doesn't it?"

"Go with the flow, as we used to say." He touched the top of my head with his lips. It didn't feel like a lover's gesture.

Loco Larry was smoking on the stoop in his combat fatigues.

"Will you be okay?" Fred asked.

I nodded. "It's a two-melatonin night."

"Sweet dreams," Larry snickered from the dark stoop.

That night, and the next night, and the next, I dreamed of Jess DuPree's leap. I dove into a rough, vast sky of implacable indigo. The dream sky thickened and roiled, like oceans churned by typhoons. I hit the sea-sky headfirst, heard the clumsy crack of bone, felt the cozy warmth of blood, tasted the sandy grit of earth, saw fluttery shadows of leaves in a tiny circle of light.

Loco Larry must have heard me pacing. He had the room below mine. On my third insomniac night, he knocked on the door. "You at war with yourself, babe?" He never waited for answers. "You know the worst part? The worst part of that war is *things.*"

I didn't mind listening; he had Seconal and Mandrax to sell as well as custom-painted signs. Better Larry make money off my nightmare than a shrink.

Things meant wadded, balled-up paper blowing in the street; it meant stiff, straight lines wrinkled with suspicious bulges; it meant disorder. Whatever was where it shouldn't be, or wasn't where you expected it to be or where it should be. Larry was the only person I knew who expected perfect order, who banked on it, who would have been happy living inside a Swiss cuckoo clock. Anything that wasn't exactly where it should be or wasn't precisely where you left it or didn't follow clean right angles was a *thing*, a death-in-waiting. The noise of panic travels up as well as down. I'd heard his screams in the night and, once, a shot. He'd terminated—that's the word he used—a plastic Kodak canister. The canister'd found its way between layers of T-shirts in his dresser drawer. Except that he'd stashed it there himself, then forgotten it. Getting forgetful was the same as inviting Death in the front door with a hearty "Howdy!"

"Things." I keep an open mind.

"Call me paranoid." Larry grinned.

"I do."

"Call me loco?"

"Some people do."

"Yeah? So if I'm loco how come the other guys didn't make it past forty and I did?"

The other guys meant Larry's band of Golden Gate campers and Haight Street panhandlers, the survivors of war who didn't make it through peace.

He had a point. He wasn't wacko, just hypersensitive to repression, extra-wired to surveillance, the way some people develop allergies to pollution or chemicals in the air.

Things were out there. Things were in him, too. One day, things would get him, but he at least could see them coming, he had night-vision implants and ESP and when all failed him he had the hairs on the back of his neck.

"That's how it's going to come, you know. A snake curled up looking just like a loop of electrical wire. Sentex inside a stray sock. A ballpoint pen someone drops on the street. A dog with an extra-wide collar. Think about that, sweetheart, they're out there. *Things* are going to get you."

He stood in the hall. I invited him in. My mother had cadged a prison-term's worth of smokes from the Gray Nuns; I was panhandling pills and consolation from a veteran.

Larry spat out his Vietnam stories. They could have been poems. He said things like "I went into *villes* scouting Charlie with twenty-twenty vision / I came out scoping Satan with the hi-res clarity of hallucination." That's more poetry than Mr. Bullock had us read. When Larry got going, his words just popped, they belonged to me as much as they did to Loco Larry, and I didn't know shit about wars or Vietnam except for the Flash kick-boxing Commies. His war poems made me mourn the major job Vietnam had done on boys like him, the tinkerers of vintage cars, the village idiots from movie-set towns with Art Deco fronts in the adobe valleys between the Coast Range and the Sierra foothills, the turban-and-sombrero country, the farmers from India, the laborers from Mexico, the crazy Armenians speeding on the shoulders raising dust and shouting insults at Okies like his old man selling corn and beans on the side of the road. All the stuff I'd picked up, all the *things*, stuck to my antennae, like pollen on a bumblebee. I didn't know shit about his California either. But I knew it was okay to be loco. There was a Bank of Craziness out there, and all I was missing was my own ATM card. It was okay to let him invite me down to his room for the sleeping pills.

"How're you intending to pay, doll? Piastres or C rations?"

"How about cash? Like running a tab?"

"How about cash, and considerations?" But he dipped
from the waist in a courtly bow as he asked and defanged
the come-on. "Yikes!" He groaned. He couldn't straighten
back up. "Arthritis."

On the ferrying-the-Styx, crossing-the-Rubicon scale,
passing behind the I ♥ MY ARSENAL sign was an 8. Inside
lay loud messages of serious derangement. Larry couldn't
keep his face scab-free or his shoelaces tied and his fly
zipped, but inside his bunker he'd bent the world to a pri-
mal schema of monochrome madness. Cleanliness counts
when you cook on a hot plate without a kitchen, wash
your dishes in the lavatory and rinse with a toilet flush. He
painted his room every day. Nightly battles with resident
bugs resulted in the ritual necessity of a decent burial and
memorial every morning. When he switched the light on,
I saw hundreds of shiny little crosses swirling up the matte
white walls and down the wood paneling. His vertical
Flanders Field of cockroach corpses. There was an open
bottle of white enamel on the sill, and a handful of
enamel-caked Q-tips.

"Wanna drink?" Larry asked. "I got muleshit whiskey."

I looked around for a place to sit. There wasn't much
furniture, just a dinette table, a wooden swivel office chair
with its back missing and a futon. And hardware. *Thing*-
busters.

Larry savored my curiosity. "You like it?" He dropped
to the floor, stretched himself flat on his stomach and
squinted into a sleek piece of weaponry.

"What is it?"

Inside every man lives a Henry Higgins. Larry described it in precise detail. A Ruger M-77 Mark II Countersniper Rifle with Leopold Varix III.3, 5x–10x variable-power tactical scope, mounted on a Harris bipod.

"Capable of serious mayhem." He beamed at me. "Did I hear yes to mule piss? And did I ever tell you about your smile?"

"What about it?" I smiled.

"What?" he asked.

He scrounged around for a clean glass or cup. I prowled his room (*a cheetah's walk*, Hari), touching his things (*a killer's hands*, Larry). I turned over ashtrays that turned out to be tape recorders, played with pens that concealed air-powered bullet-shooters, flipped through a copy or two of *Machine Gun News*. Larry was crazy for ownership. He kept mean little pyramids of knives and daggers on the floor by the futon, within easy reach. The bulkier toys he'd lined up against the walls, like gallery exhibits. I dusted a pistol crossbow with a sleeve. Some of the toys I had no names for; I hadn't ever seen them, not even in Frankie's Flash extravaganzas. I took in the bowling trophies and the war trophies lined up neatly on the dinette table. The war trophies were in jam jars: pickled mushrooms and ginseng roots labeled "Charlie Ears." I wandered into the kitchen alcove and checked out the snapshots held in place with magnets on the refrigerator door: buddies looking like summer campers grinned out of pedicabs. Okie faces, some African American faces. All of them romantics and innocents. And, all of them, fated to be victims or villains. I identified with those guys. I'd been drafted, too.

We sat with our whiskies, I on Larry's only chair, Larry on an ammo crate. He started on his stories again. Some I'd heard before, but I heard them differently that night; I heard them as Muzak in the museum of needs and loss.

He told the story of the time he'd come across a codger sleeping in his hooch, and shot him six times in the head because you never know when Charlie's dead or just playing dead. We'd warned them; we'd told them to clear out. We'd told them this was big-time pacification. And the story of the old gal fishing in a canal, just a line in the water coming out from under a broad hat, and he'd figured where her head had to be, and he'd let her have it.

You can never be sure, never get careless: that was Larry's motto. It was also the tragedy of the loco. You kill someone doing what you do all the time, like sleeping, or what you used to do, like fishing, or what you want to do, like beating off—he took out a teenaged boy once—and you can never do it again. Larry could be rolling in proteins, fishing off the shallows, but every time he saw a fisherman the big, round peasant hat bobbed and teased, daring him to line up its center like a bull's-eye. And if Larry could line up, so could someone else. I learned the lesson Larry was teaching. *Things are out there.* The war Ham had protested wasn't the war that Larry had fought.

"How about those sleepy pills you offered?"

"I have a better idea," Larry said. He pulled me up off the chair without the back. "Wanna dance?" He didn't ask it as a question. We stumbled around the room in a clumsy foxtrot a couple of times.

"Not tonight," I said.

He loosened his grip. "Let's have a kiss then." He pressed my face into his.

"Not tonight, Larry."

"Sumbitch!" But he let go of me.

On the Seconal, I got a great deal.

Ham and Larry. Larry and Ham. I spent a lot of time with each of them, because I wanted to. It wasn't about sex, and it wasn't about self-discovery as it had been with Frankie. Frankie'd looked exotic, but acted familiar. Ham and Larry were harder for me to read. They were the true exotics, coming of age as they'd done in contrary times. Larry'd napalmed villages; Ham'd impresarioed love-ins. And Bio-Mom? She'd embroiled herself and me in messy mysteries.

Like Ham and Larry, she would be in her fifties now. She must have started out romantic, must have floated into the sixties in a haze of sex, drugs and the sanctity of rebellion. Then the war had snuck up on her as it had on Larry and Ham, an apocalypse segregating hawks from doves, cynics from idealists, setting up areas where women couldn't follow. Vietnam had plucked a slow, shy kid from a Central Valley farm and provided him paranoia and cheap arms. Peace had coarsened a draft resister to deal maker on the minibudget Bay Area film circuit. We know how our men had reacted. Vietnam had been their central experience—you couldn't escape their blasted faces on the streets—they'd coped or they'd been gutted. War had blessed them with terrible clarity.

But what about the women? What about that flower fräulein, Bio-Mom? Should I envy the mother who had put her bad karma behind her in an Indian prison, dumped her bastard child on Hindi-speaking nuns and moved on? She'd done what'd felt good, what'd felt right at the time, and consequences be damned.

For her and Ham as much as for Larry, Vietnam ended on the roof of the U.S. Embassy in Saigon. Scramble into choppers, then pull up the ladders! Teach the Statue of Liberty to catch up to speed!

But what about us, Vietnam's war-bastards and democracy's love children? We're still coping with what they did, what they saw, what they salvaged, what they mangled and dumped on that Saigon rooftop that maniacal afternoon.

I quit my cocktail-waitressing job in midshift the night Fred Pointer came into the club looking as though he'd wandered in from a Mylanta ad.

Fred ordered a glass of house red and shoved an airmail envelope in my face. I didn't grab the envelope from him. The more nowhere a country, the prettier its stamps: been-everywhere Frankie'd taught me that. The stamps of dingy, deforested, microscopic hills with the Indian post-mark on Fred's envelope weren't exotic, which meant India saw itself as a world power. That cheered me. I con-centrated on the stamps. Saplings sprouted out of the brown hills. I felt the universe was communicating mes-sages of hope to me.

I brought Fred his glass of Cabernet Sauvignon from the bar, and sidled in beside him on the banquette. Beth was tending bar that night. She aimed one of her go-slow-on-the-fraternization frowns at us. "Cheers." I raised an imaginary glass.

Fred stretched his legs out under the table. The legs were very long. The Gucci loafers stuck way out into the aisle. "Are those Mona Lisas on your socks?" I asked by way of small talk.

Fred peered at his own feet, amazed. He lifted them a foot off the floor. "Aliens have begun a slow takeover of my body," he said.

"Don't do this to yourself, Fred."

"I don't have to. Jess is doing it for me."

"Jealousy doesn't suit you. I'm not giving Ham a hard time about . . ."

I stopped myself before I said, "Jess." What happened at Vito's between them, the circumstances that made me leave Ham on the dance floor and cadge a ride home with Fred that night, whatever mean streak made me even consider punishing Ham and Jess by seducing Fred, those feelings were unworthy of me. I wasn't a victim and I wouldn't become a codependent. Jesus, Mama DiMartino used to say, made a cornerstone of the very stone that builders had the dumbness to reject. Matthew 21:22: *The one who falls on this stone will be broken to pieces; and it will crush anyone on whom it falls.* I needed Fred's help. Which meant I had to stop his world from caving in on him.

Kiki, the waitress I was closest to, scowled as she hurried past our table with a tray of margaritas. *Get the slob to buy expensive cocktails or get back to your station.* I flashed Kiki inscrutability.

"Remember that night at Vito's?" Fred asked.

"The night of the beginning of your misery?"

"Remember what I said that night?"

"You said a lot of things. We both did. We spilled our guts, we philosophized about black holes and peripheries—"

He stopped me. "About gumshoeing."

I didn't remember.

"Facts are facts." He tapped the edge of the table with the envelope. "Accuracy doesn't mean shit. You have to ask the right questions."

"And you've asked them?" I held my hand out for the envelope. I had a right to know.

"Cops and hacks ask, What does it mean, where's the payoff?"

"And what does the smart-ass PI ask?"

"Fred Pointer's smart, not smart-ass. Fred doesn't solve mysteries; he unsolves them. Every fucking case is a moral quest."

I snatched the envelope—*a thing*, as Larry'd say—from Fred. Larry's vision was like a plague, and I'd caught it. We were both *thing-dodgers* now. We'd be lost without *things*.

The sender of this *thing* had used a manual typewriter. The individual letters in the words didn't quite line up right. Some keys had been hit harder than others. The *F* for "Fred" and the *V* for "Vulture" for instance, were darker than the *P* and the *o* in "Pointer." The only manual typewriters I'd ever seen were on reruns of sitcoms Mama'd watched. It wasn't about detection and deduction. I was taking my own advice to Fred from that Vito's night, and working the peripheries. The center's a sinkhole.

In the envelope was more dirt the Bombay investigator had dug up and euphemistically titled: *Report of Continuing Investigation.*

> Subsequent to the unauthorized examination of the orphanage files, a thorough search was conducted into court

documents of Jaipur, Rajasthan State, India, of the period
1968 through 1977, specifically into those documents that
pertained to the adjudication of criminal cases involving
Caucasian tourists of the female sex. A further narrowing
of this category was made in terms of location of crime.
Only two apprehended Caucasian females were found to
have been convicted of, or indicted for, unlawful activities
in Ranipur, Laxmipur and Panagad villages. These villages
are situated within a morning's bus ride from Devigaon,
that site to which reference was made by Hari, *chowkidar.*

Speculation has no place in this report. Nevertheless, it
should be borne in mind that a top-level inquiry is
presently being mounted by the opposition party in the
Lok Sabha house of the Indian Parliament regarding the
death in prison last month of the Eurasian male felon
against whom the said Caucasian female had deposed in
court and which deposition had led to the conviction and
the sentencing of the deceased.

"I'm sorry to bring lousy news," Fred mumbled.

I said, "I didn't know him, Fred. I don't have a right to
be upset."

Bio-Dad had no liens on my heart. The strangler's
palms caressed my throat, fingers tightened and twisted.
Dry coughs and cries escaped.

"How did he die? Does your man in Bombay say anything about what he died of?"

Fred buried his head in his hands. "I don't know."

"He was *my* father, Fred. I'm not mourning him. He
didn't earn the right to be mourned."

True despair has halogen wattage. Fred's face could
have lit up Doomsday. "The two Caucasian females in the
report? One of them's someone I know."

A redhead in a sequined vintage prom dress veered wide of Fred's Guccis on her way to the restroom. The redhead had perfected the Marilyn Monroe hip swivel. I watched her vanish into the men's room.

"What! You know my mother?"

"There's a fifty-fifty chance that I know your mother."

"Okay. Who is she?"

"Devi—or whatever your name is—you're just an upstate girl who got in over her head. And you're dragging us all into it . . ." He let it drop. Then, just as suddenly after clearing his throat, he became all business. I sat primly, all client.

"Your mother could be Jess DuPree of this city, currently doing million-dollar-plus business as CEO of a hot author-escorting agency. I showed Jess a copy of a courtroom transcript Rajeev sent, and she said, 'Sweetdick, go fuck the Golden Gate, will you?' "

In the nightmare I could ease only with Loco Larry's barbiturates, Jess's ghost stole my lithe, living body, then coaxed it to dive off the bridge and drown itself. In life, I *was* the ghost; I'd already haunted a whole village.

Deforested hills can be replanted. Vision is will. I quit the club job before my shift was over so I could focus on Getting Jess.

The next morning I worked on Ham. He invited me on a two-day location shoot somewhere in the redwoods. Up there in the Sierras, I sprung my politically correct scheme on him; once Berkeley, always Berkeley. "It must be the mountains, but it's just dawned on me. I'm taking work away from aliens. You don't have to speak English to wait tables at the club."

He closed his eyes, inhaled the wholesome woodsy smells, and went through a list of people with businesses other than restaurants and nightclubs who owed him big. Jess DuPree wasn't on that list. I pushed my case as a safe driver with *mucho* charm and *muy mucho* personality. Jess's agency, I reminded him, was always looking for drivers at short notice.

"But what do you know about escorting authors?"

"They're writers, not authors, Ham! They're meat puppets with autographing pens. Escorting's a simple pickup and delivery system."

"Don't tell Jess you're planning to model yourself on the UPS lady."

Ham called Jess on his cell phone. I was hired before I got back to the city.

E.T., get off the pay phone. Hi, Mom! I'm the infant you mislaid.

What had I expected to find in my mother's museum? Harem pants and killing tools? Baby clothes and toys?

Give me a sign, Bio-Mom.

Jess's agency occupied the upper floor of a two-story house on Clay off Presidio. The walls were painted in combinations of colors that I hadn't crayoned with in my Crayola days in Schenectady. Puce, chartreuse, fraise, gamboge. All the sofas were shrouded in red and black kilims. The camel harnesses on the floor were meant to be sat on. Wool shawls embroidered with paisleys hung in place of blinds or drapes in the windows. All ledges, sills and tabletops were cluttered with brass gods, mirrored elephants, copper urns, lacquered boxes, sandalwood beads and stone eggs on tarnished trays. This wasn't California. It wasn't even America.

Jess caught my look, and reacted defensively. "Don't judge *me*, Ms. Fresh-from-Schenectady! I *went* to Asia with a pierced nose. I was the first one to try a nose ring in Berkeley." She strode ahead of me, a brisk, jowly, touched-up blonde in Armani pants.

"No tips in this job," she went on. "Only egomaniacs for clients. Still want it?" She went through an archway hung with a mirrored valance into a small, interconnecting room, and I followed. "If you do, this is the HQ of the world's best MEs."

I took in the conventional office furniture and equipment: desks, filing cabinets, computers, a printer, a fax machine, a copier. No organizer or dossier for the tidy storage of maternal feelings.

"We call this the Wall," she said. The wall behind her desk was hung with head shots of celebrity authors.

Yeah? As in Loco Larry's?

She sat at her desk, sizing me up more frankly than she had at Dahlia's Divan.

No desk clutter of pens, paper clips, rubber bands; no family photographs; no flowers; no smiling faces doodled on scratch pads; no framed fortune-cookie-Confucian proverbs. Only one item out of place in that Office Depot decor: an antique wooden lap desk that scribes in another era on another continent must have squatted at.

She caught me being distracted by the lap desk. "From a Muslim slum in Bombay. India's one great junkyard."

"I know." I am capable of micronostalgia. "A guy I used to date back east called India hot, loud, filthy, smelly, the Club Med of choice for druggies and convicts on the lam."

"Rubbish!" Jess snapped. "A typical white male. You have to open yourself up to ancient cultures. You go to a junkyard only because you know it's full of tossed-out treasures."

Wha, Mom?

She pointed a pencil at the Wall, and popped her interview question. "How many clients can you identify?"

I chose the chair farthest from the wall hung with framed book jackets and autographed portraits. It reminded me of Dan's Diner in Saratoga Springs, where you couldn't see the wall because of signed glossies of old vaudeville stars no one knew or cared about anymore. The

Flash's winning trick was to never let the enemy see him sweat. "I love tests," I said. I didn't leave my chair. In the past year I'd read three vampire novels and half of a Stephen King. I'd caught Grisham and Waller on morning shows on network TV, but that didn't mean I'd recognize them if they were on the Wall.

"A joke, not a test. Ham doesn't hang out with dummies." She pulled a thick ring-binder out of a drawer, and held it out to me. She obviously did arm curls with serious weights. If I wanted to tussle with her, I'd have to pump up.

I moved to a chair across from Jess, and flipped through the binder. Mug shots of writers; press releases from their publishers.

Jess launched into the dos and don'ts of "ME-ing":

Make sure your watch battery doesn't die on you.

Check the map and plot your route from hotel to radio/TV stations, bookstores, et cetera, the night before.

Make nice to hotel doormen and valet parking attendants.

Keep a care basket visible in the backseat. Refill supply of bottled waters, fruits, candies, tea bags.

Hide an emergency kit of condoms, antacids, Gas-X, Ex-Lax, et cetera. Offer traveling iron, curling iron, if necessary, prior to TV interview and photo shoot.

Have quarters and dollar bills handy for tollbooths.

Ask for, and hang on to, all receipts.

Don't yak about yourself. A ME doesn't have personal problems. A ME doesn't have a life. Your client's got enough for everyone, or thinks he does.

If your author is a lech, use your head before your muscle.

Have fun. Even the shits don't stay around longer than two days.

I played it her way. *Got it, boss!* I even improvised additions out loud to her blue-book of dos and don'ts:

Keep file cards on each client's likes and dislikes. A ME shouldn't have to ask, Do you take it black, straight, rare, imported, domestic? Keep your private Yellow Pages of where to buy after-hours liquor, finest-human-hair-wig-at-shortest-notice, et cetera. Practice the Heimlich maneuver. Cultivate a shrink and/or dealer for emergency requests.

"Forget the pills," Jess snapped. She stalked off to the window to look out on caffeine-deprived San Franciscans hurrying into Middle Grounds.

"Just a joke," I apologized, "not a business proposition." I filed her overreaction.

Jess swung around on her designer flats. "Hilarious," she said.

I watched and heard her take two deep breaths, and focus on serenity. Serenity has to sneak up on you, shock you. I could have taught her that, but she wasn't ready to be a pupil. There's only the willingness to prey or be preyed on.

"I'll give you Stark Swann to cut your teeth on. He'll test your sense of humor."

"Is that a male or a female?"

"Is that another joke?" She made her way to the fax machine, which was spewing out changes in the itinerary of an Astro Sense Publishing House author. "They've lined up more interviews for Ma Varuna. The New Age types have fat wallets."

"It's a question." I'd never heard of either of those authors, but I was glad I was getting a client who'd press my patience button instead of faith. "Hey, give me a break, I'm a very quick study."

"Well, study this. Go into any drugstore. Check out the book rack. *The Chartreuse Night* and *The Burglar Bliss* are out there with the beta-blockers."

The Palest Poison was number seven on the lists that counted, and still climbing. She frisbeed a scarlet-and-gold promo kit at me. My reflexes are sharp; she should have guessed. Stark Swann had to be one vain dude. A jock with a chiseled jaw and styled silver hair brooded on the mysteries of prefab Nature.

"Nervous?" she asked.

"Should I be?"

"Let's get a mineral water and find out."

Nervous only like a squadron leader going into battle. Logistics, contour maps, streets to master: San Francisco as house-to-house combat. I had buildings and parking lots to locate on the city map, shortcuts to plot.

"Okay," I heard myself say. I wanted to say, *Hey, you're a widow! Daddy's dead, no fear he'll pop up and ruin your life. We know what men who've shared the same woman are like, but what are women who've shared the same man like?* I led the way to the Middle Grounds.

There in the smart, bright, busy neighborhood hangout, with music from an FM station piped overhead and thumbed paperbacks of Calvino and Eco on tabletops, I learned the story of one such woman. Jess presented it as her invitation to concubinely bonding; I heard it as a cautionary tale against mindless passion.

Jess had dropped out of Baba Lalji's ashram and dropped into Asia in the late fall of 1968. She had hit all the usual hippie highs and lows in the next six years, and then it had happened. Karma, she called it. Her karma revealed itself in a village named Laxmipur. The year was 1974, Jess twenty-eight.

Where's that? Give me a country. A quadrant. Desert or jungle. Wet or dry.

What does it matter? It happened. It happened in a season so dry the soil cracks open wide enough to swallow dying cattle and children.

All right, so Jess was twenty-eight, the war was over and back in America the bile was receding, but in a village where the wells were choked with bodies and the fields aged like bruises, yellow-brown, it was still hard to be an American and a romantic.

And how do you protest the war by doing dope on an alien continent? That didn't make sense.

It had to Jess in her twenties; still did. It made all the sense in the world to anyone her age, Ham's age, Fred's age, those who had survived and owned up to what the war'd really done for them, how it'd freed them to be themselves, to curse and fuck and burn and loot, to kill or die, to feel superior while having fun. The war didn't change you, that was Jess's point. The war leveled the playing field for girls like her. When she talked of her hopeless childhood out in Fresno, I thought: *Whoa! That's Grandma and Gramps!*

"Why are you always smiling?" she demanded.

"It's so *fascinating!*" I said.

Jess'd overlanded to India shortly after she'd broken up with Ham. There, she got that out of the way. I admired her directness, and added, funny thing about Ham, wasn't it, that he couldn't let go of his women, he needed to hang on to every last one of them. Jess relaxed. She said, Yeah, the exes, the one-night stands, even the nut who shaved her head for him.

The one with the hat at Vito's?

The trouble was that Ham's wildness was Berkeley wildness. Jess sighed. A familiar wildness. The same with the Haight. A sad, shabby, funky, show-offy Look-Ma-Number-One kind of wildness. You had to leave the country, chuck logic, fuck reason, screw Enlightenment if you wanted more than that.

Translated into Fonglish, Jess was confessing to a bad case of *needs*.

Young Jess made her way through England and France, Greece and Turkey and Afghanistan, sharing rides with the world's waifs, strays, seekers, sickos, sensualists, and stopped for a while in the Indian village of Laxmipur in a rainless month. She tossed her backpack on the blistered soil, lay down under a shade tree with brittle, wrinkled leaves, looked into a sky sheer as muslin and recited in a voice that was sure and strong.

" 'Zero at the bone,' " she said.

"Dickinson," I exclaimed. "Isn't it?"

"You *are* a quick study." She ordered lattes. "They should ration such moments. One per lifetime."

"Mr. Bullock, he was my English teacher back east, he was big on Frost too."

Jess was back under the muslin-thin sky in Laxmipur, communing with Emily Dickinson.

" 'The Grass divides as with a Comb / A spotted shaft is seen,' and wham! There was this . . . *apparition!*"

She *invoked* this *thing*, this snake-*thing*. This snake-god or snake-devil, whatever it was, just rose right out of the cracks in the dry soil and rocked her in his arms.

A trip?

"You had to have been there, Devi! There's no describing that erotic moment."

My beginning, I thought. *I've just heard my beginning.*

I heard her say, "Just no describing how erotic it was! I was a poetry-mad kid, I thought I was going to be the Emily of Fresno, can you imagine that? Poetry was my god, before that man . . ."

I *saw* what Jess'd *felt*. My father—her god, my devil—rocked her in his arms. I concentrated on those non-human arms. On their litheness. On their strength and meanness. On the starlight luster of his killer hands. Prince of Darkness. Prince Materializing out of Darkness. He didn't have to touch her. I was wantonness waiting to happen.

"Meaning, he made you happy?"

Jess tuned in to my wavelength. "He made me wanton."

That was her exact phrase. Happiness is the consolation prize. Suddenly I understood, without wanting to, why I had run away from Frankie Fong. One day soon, my god would touch down. My breathing would tighten. I would thrill to the shudder of Zero in my spine.

It turned out that I had to cut more than my teeth on Stark Swann.

Starkie Boy was first off the plane. First class; aisle seat; probably bulkhead to show off those long, smug legs in blue denim. ("*Your* writers will always be first off," Jess'd confided. "Even if the publisher stuck them with economy, they'll push their way to the front.") From the way the Asian flight attendant was creaming as she smiled her "Have a happy rest of vacation, Mr. Swann," I figured at least one of Jess's tips would come in handy.

People at the gate—the limo drivers with Velcro signboards, escorts from hotels, businesses and universities—all took a second glance. *You're sure you're not mine?* He was good-looking, but it wasn't that. It wasn't his clothes either: denim shirt, bone-and-turquoise beads, turquoise belt buckle, blue antelope-skin boots. No, it had to do with his bearing. He stood, he strode, he scanned, did all the things we do except for the autographing, but with the *solipsism*, there's just no other word for it, of people out of *People* magazine. A celebrity *is*. The infamous have to strut to get noticed, and the evil slink away so they won't be noticed. Swann didn't care one way or another. He didn't have to. He was the center of his universe.

I held up my promo copy of *The Palest Poison* high above the heads of his groupies. "Hi," I shouted, "I'm Devi Dee. How was the flight?"

He pen-wielded his way to me. The pen was a top-of-the-line Mont Blanc. "You want me to write in your name, Miss Gorgeous Smile? I'm in a fab mood, take advantage of me."

"Devi from Leave It to Me." I pulled his three-page itinerary from inside my promo copy.

"Where's Jess? She always meets me. What's this, I don't rate her anymore?"

When I angled for the agency job, it was just so I could bloodhound Bio-Mom. Expanding my knowledge of human psychology was a bonus. "You'll have to take that up with her," I said. "Meanwhile, I thought we could first drive to your hotel, then have a bite if you're hungry, stop by some bookstores if you're not too tired or do whatever else you'd rather do before your print interviews this afternoon—all the TV stuff's tomorrow, as you know from the itinerary—and then leave around six for the bookstore in Marin. Only if all this sounds okay to you, of course." I held my hand out for his laptop in its Targus case. The laptop was lighter than the other two carry-ons. "I should have thought of having a cart handy. Sorry."

Swann thrust his garment bag at me instead. "Nobody but *moi* touches my moody machine." Then he turned silky on me. "I'll need a little sewing and pressing done right away. When's the first interview? I don't think there's enough time for housekeeping to take care of it. Would you mind? And did you book Hideo-*san* for my shiatsu?"

. . .

I left Stark Swann meditating in the lotus position on the floor of his suite at the Stanford Court. The lotus position was his fail-safe cure for jet lag. To me, he looked just like another cowboy with hemorrhoids. While he meditated, I ordered flowers to be delivered to the suite in Jess's name and forged a personal note, made the appointment with the masseur named Hideo, dashed down to where the Corolla was valet parked for the emergency kit that included needle, thread and buttons, steamed wrinkles out of his jacket and my skirt, checked in for changes in itinerary, confirmed the afternoon's print interview *and* still had time left to flirt with Ham over a double espresso.

"Oh, boy!" Ham laughed. "Why am I thinking *All About Eve* all of a sudden? If I were Jess, I'd be scared."

He read me wrong. I didn't want to be read at all. "If I screw up in the job, I'd be letting you down. Jess hired me because of you." Oh, I was good.

Ham was satisfied; why burden him with truth? Jess was a stand-in, nothing more. *He made me wanton.* Only this time, sitting in a coffeehouse in North Beach, I heard her words as a plea. It wasn't my fault, he was a natural force, a calamity, an act of God. A typhoon had touched down, blasted the body and flattened the soul. I got what I needed from the memory. Some are born wanton; others are born weak and made wanton. *I am wanton.* I kissed Ham lightly on the lips. Poor Ham.

The journalist from *Bay Style/Bay View* was a punctual woman in pastels. I ordered a macrobiotic salad and

Evian for Starkie Boy, black coffee for her, nothing for me from room service, then shrunk into myself on the love seat to recoup.

The journalist had a mean streak. As her first question, she asked, "Why do you write these romances? Just for the money?"

"Excuse me?" The romance writer didn't have an answer ready, but I don't think it a ME's job to come to his rescue.

"Mind you, I'm not against you making money." The journalist tapped her tape recorder. It was working. "Not if you give some of it away. I was in the Peace Corps way back when Americans cared about the world. You want to know where I was? In Brazil. No Carnival where I was. You see these hands? Kids starved to death in them." She held up her hands.

They were moisturized and manicured. I'd never have connected those hands with Brazilian street kids. You never know. *Things* are out there, like land mines. Even in an expensive suite at a hotel like the Stanford Court.

Starkie Boy surprised me. "You didn't have to go to Brazil." His voice was sad, soft, forgiving. He strode across the room on those splendid antelope-skin boots. "You should have come to the Swann shack instead." He painted a central Florida childhood of hunger and beatings. His father must have been a nasty drunk. Some days he was so starved he'd gorged himself on live bait, knowing he'd be belted for not bringing a catch home. The romances he wrote as a tribute to his mother, to all the brave women like her who deserved better, who deserved the happy, fulfilled lives he gave his heroines. Hacks wrote for fat advances. He wrote to make reparations for what men did to women.

I'd read his promo kit. He hadn't made up the Florida childhood. He'd grown up in Stark. And he'd gone back to Florida—to Gainesville and Orlando—for a couple of visiting-writer stints. There was nothing about abusive dads and worm diets in the publicity material, nothing about damage and despair. I warmed to him, in spite of his beads and his spray-stiffened coiffure. I saw the journalist out the door with a crisp "And when will it appear in *Bay Style/Bay View?*"

Swann shouldn't have soured these feelings. I closed the door, and he said, "Frustrated lez bitch! She needs a hot-beef injection. If she hadn't been a dawg, I'd have administered it, too."

Zip it up, Starkie Boy!

That night in a packed bookstore in Marin, Stark Swann read from the first chapter of his new novel. On the microphone, his voice took on a low-decibel roughness and sincerity. It made you picture red barns, cornfields, grazing Herefords. I saw the weathered planks as he read, felt splinters sting a naked toe. Oh, Clint Eastwood, you should have been there. To the audience, you already were. I forced myself to stop listening, and count heads in that crowded store. The head count was part of a ME's job. The bookstore would report on the number of units sold.

Sometimes, like when Fate's croupier fixes the throw, and the suety slob in the white suit pockets your dice, and

Lawman Lance weighs in with low blows, and the burned-out bimbo you saved from rape runs off with the finicky florist from Sacramento, there's only one way to go: just suck it in and spur your tired mare on on the hot, dusty, cruel trail home, 'cos there's a sweet, sad-eyed woman waitin' for you by the kitchen stove, a loving woman who knows you and cares for you, a real woman who understands you so well she doesn't shackle your ankles to the bedpost but gives her blissful womanhood to you of her own accord and for as long as you need and want her to, and who senses when to step aside, and lets you go without tears, and weeps only after the dust's blown . . .

That's when I stopped the head count. Swann groupies writhed in their seats. I was witnessing a feeding frenzy. I was hearing a refrain: *He made me wanton.* I understood the apparition Jess'd confessed to at the Middle Grounds. A romance writer, like Starkie Boy, had inspired Jess's tropical fantasy about a sweaty night of love with an alien god. Emily Dickinson had been an excuse. Bio-Mom had scripted her life—and mine—on a romance novel off a rack. I hated Starkie Boy for not telling the whole tale, the part about what happens after the dust clears, and the child is strangled. I need the world to connect Starkie Boy with vultures tearing flesh off a corpse's bruised throat.

My voice; I suddenly understood, the sexy nun's voice, graveled by scar tissue.

That's why I agreed to the glass of wine in his room. He said, "Come in for a drink? Help me unwind? I hate hotels, they're so sterile." It didn't qualify as a hitting-on-me situation. Let's just say he facilitated what I planned to do.

I accepted the invitation. I went with him to the bar and sipped a Chardonnay because I wanted to. Then I rode the elevator to his floor, led the way into his suite, let him pour minibar brandy into two snifters, let him undress me before I undressed him. That night, nobody made me do anything I didn't want to do. I slow-paraded my nakedness and watched him twitch and harden. Enthrallment is an exquisite instrument of pain. When it comes to enthralling, I am a natural. Which was why he didn't see me shake too much Mandrax (thanks, Larry!) into his snifter, didn't taste it on his greedy tongue, and after a while didn't feel me pleasure him. And just before he passed out, I had him roll over and lie on his stomach, and when he was out so cold he wouldn't feel the tickle of the K-bar knifepoint (thanks again, Larry!), I nicked an endearment on his left buttock: cw. My homage to my neighborhood *graffitiste*, Cee-Double-You. Because that's what the women *who give of their blissful selves of their own accord and for as long as you want them to*, the real women, do.

The night I was practicing K-bar calligraphy on Starkie Boy, Fred Pointer was jogging to his death. I imagine connections everywhere; more of them are nooses than bridges.

Fred's life changed after our last meeting at Steep Steps. He became accident-prone, pulled a pectoral on a bench press, sprained his ankle on a golf swing, burned his hand on the car radiator. *Things.* There are things out there waiting to zap you. Unguardedness may prove fatal. In Fred's case it did. A woman walking her black Lab in Land's End by the Sutro Baths found a badly charred body under a cypress tree. Like Rajeev Raj, like Madame Kezarina, I find signs all around me. The papers called it an accident, but Fred committed suttee. Fred's despair burned as brightly as a funeral pyre.

Fred made better than the obit page in the local papers. The way he died made him news. *Accident or Homicide?* Two national tabloids picked up the death. I read *Bay Area Private Eye Slain by Viet Gang of San Jose* at Walgreens, and *San Francisco Gumshoe Molested by Aliens from Outer Space* at Safeway.

The coroner's report was later leaked to the press by a lab assistant with a cash-flow problem. Fred's blood showed an alcohol level of .072 and the presence of an unidentified vegetal poison that was being sent outside the United States for more tests.

Why do I dream of Fred's corpse instead of Fred the way he was at Vito's or Steep Steps or the Boss Bean? The corpse floats in the shallow pool of rainwater in the sad ruins. No face, a *thing*: bloated, naked, rock-scraped.

Through Fred's death, I learned something new about Berkeley. Not about Berkeley the scuzzy city north of Oakland in the East Bay, menaced by fault lines every which way—a West Coast Troy or Rensselaer, if you like, though with many more sari shops and satay houses; and with many, many more panhandlers, street vendors, pistol-whippers, performance artists and prophets in drag; with fancier mansions in fire-prone hills and, in the lower flats, tackier adobe holding pens—but about the *space* that Ham and his friends inhabited.

Berkeley, I began to understand at the wake Ham held for Fred on *Last Chance*, was a kind of fraternity, a marine unit, all-for-one, one-for-all, teammates-for-life bonding experience, it was the you-had-to-have-been-there, you-had-to-have-seen-it place, something I was too young for, too late for, and would never appreciate. It was the only place in America where it could be taken for granted that everyone over thirty, say, had slept with everyone else over thirty. But *that* Berkeley was no more, gone the way people back east talked of old Manhattan. That Berkeley was as much a time as a site: it was a time of dark possibility, discovery and forgiveness.

Ham was Mr. Berkeley, that Berkeley. He was its center. And because of his Berkeley training, he got along with street people like the Stoop Man and the Duvet Man and Devi the Waif, and still lived on a houseboat in Sausalito and picked up women half his age. Because he was Berkeley, he took people in, gave panhandlers five-dollar bills, served AIDS lunches, boycotted more kinds of food than I'd ever eaten. He, Jess and Fred had marched for peace, for civil rights, for women, gays, migrants, had gone to jail, signed petitions, run for city councils, run radical campaigns. And now they also drove big cars, lived large lives, flew business class, ate at the best restaurants, drank the best wines, took massages, ski trips, private cruises. They climbed together, deep-sea dove and white-water rafted together. It was their community-hedonist thing. Food, revolution, sex, art, ecology, drugs, music, books, writers, films. Epicures, sensualists. They cozied with movie stars, politicians, best-selling writers under *fatwa*, but it wasn't a big deal to them. Berkeley might be the Harvard of the West Coast, but it didn't empower them to assume arrogance. They kept a low profile. Harvard taught its graduates that the rest of the world was inept and waiting for them to take over; Berkeley taught that the world was a cool place and shouldn't be disturbed.

Ham took charge and produced the wake as a little folk, a little punk, a little gospel-rock catharsis extravaganza. The music: Peter, Paul and Mary; Pete Seeger. The flowers: Lilies in mourners' hair. Cremation: Blessed and switched on by a Buddhist priest named Steve Lama. Scattering of ashes: After a two-hour hike and off a Point Reyes promontory.

The powdered corpse played with seals and sea lions.

Vietnam wasn't a war; it was a divide. On one side, the self-involved idealists; on the other, we the napalm-scarred kids. In between, a country that elected leaders, who got boys like Larry to pull the triggers.

After the hike, the select few, among them the ex-lover who'd shaved her head—Ham kept A and B lists—ended up on his houseboat in Sausalito. The way they grieved wasn't familiar. Where I wept, got drunk and started songs I didn't know the words to, they hugged, they smoked, they groped, they melted into an intimacy that was physical. One image that stays with me from that evening: the Hairless Hat-Wearer, wearing the wispy dress I'd clowned in in Dahlia's shop the first time I'd run into Jess, danced the Seven Veils in the galley kitchen, and when she finished, she grabbed a pasta-serving platter and asked Ham to deliver her his head. Ham couldn't console the hatless woman just then, because he was consoling Jess. I was sober enough not to confuse hugs and pats with grabs and gropes. The soft scrape of lips, the shucking off of loafers, the peeling off of sticky shirts: I heard the sweet, low moans of invitation and acceptance.

I didn't exist. I might as well have never existed. That snake-*thing* had been a Dickinson wanna-be's fantasy.

Ham pushed open the door to the lavatory, guided Jess in, then kicked the door to shut it behind them. The door didn't swing back all the way. I could have closed it; I should have walked away. I didn't have to watch my mother and my lover make love in the cramped loo of a houseboat in Marin. I saw her legs straight out, a flash of Ham's blue Jockeys. Mother Steals Daughter's Boyfriend belongs on *The Jenny Jones Show.*

I stayed rooted; I stared; I envied.

This has to be serenity.

Jess and Ham inhabited space where all actions were guiltless, all feelings natural.

And when I couldn't stand watching my lover and my mother go at it any longer, I fuzz-busted all the way from Sausalito to Beulah Street, stole a parking space from a tourist's Beamer, rushed to Loco Larry's apartment.

"What freaked you out, doll?" His bulked-up torso blocked the I ♥ MY ARSENAL sign on the opened door. He had a beer in his hand. Empties lined up along the sides of the futon. Drunk enough to hope his luck had changed. "A beer? Grass? Nookie?"

"I'm not a couch potato. The evening deserves better."

He took it as we'll-fuck-later. *"No problema, señorita."* He grinned. *"No* fucking *problema.* We'll get in the Larry-mobile and drive around a bit." He checked the pockets of his fatigues for the keys to his truck.

The keys had to be in the left pocket of the windbreaker hanging from a peg just inside the front door—I could make out a lumpy sag that looked car-keys size—but hanging with Larry meant accommodating the macho locked inside the loco.

"If you're in the mood, let's go do some serious gardening." He clicked his crepe-soled heels and let me in. "Let's fucking garden till we drop."

I hadn't figured Larry as a green thumb. There were no potted plants on his windowsills, not even marijuana under artificial lighting in his closet.

He stripped off the fatigues he had on, down to his plaid boxer shorts, no explanations, then pulled on fatigues exactly like the ones he'd just taken off. "Help yourself to a beer," he ordered. He opened the apartment door, and swaggered off to the bathroom in the hall. I followed, because he didn't say no. The top shelf of the bathroom cabinet held the greasepaint he was looking for. I watched him daub on battle-ready black.

"Great gardener look," I joked.

We ambled back to his apartment. One of the Somali kids stuck his head in the open door. "Scoot!" Larry barked, but he tossed the kid a half-used-up roll of Certs. When we were finally ready for the road, he had on a camouflage helmet and jackboots. Any guy who'd poop-scooped shredded buddy-flesh in paddy fields on the other side of the moon was entitled. Larry *looked* wired; I *felt* it.

"The bulbs for planting are in the truck." He grinned. "When apocalypse hits, we dig up what we sowed. That's the plan."

Whatever the plan, I didn't get it. "Sweets, put yourself in Robinson Crusoe's shoes."

"Crusoe lost his shoes when his ship went down."

Larry tried again, a good sport. "What's the one must-have item on a desert island?"

"A sun-powered TV?"

He thumped my arm, buddy fashion. "An arsenal in weatherproof storage underground." He pulled a dolly out of a cluttered corner of the kitchen alcove, and started to pile up crates, canisters, cache tubes. "Yours truly's partial to AK-47s and Colt AR15HBARs."

Forget *The Victory Garden*; tune out *Martha Stewart Living*. Larry's gardening was for survivalists who relied on more than organic flowers and vegetables for their postapocalypse days.

I was Larry's buddy; I took a shot at wheeling the loaded dolly closer to the apartment door. The dolly didn't move, but pain did, and that pain settled in the small of my back in one burning, bouncing ball.

"Hey, forget that." He grinned. "You bring the ammo. I got me the genuine article. Steel cored, with mega mayhem capacity." He handed me a heavy-enough box. I locked up after us, and lugged the box to where Larry's panel truck was parked, in front of a fire hydrant a block and a half away on Cole.

Larry had a right to think his luck had changed for the better. The truck hadn't been ticketed. The only paper under the windshield wiper was a flyer for a new Shabazz Bakery.

We loaded our gardening equipment and the dolly into the back of the truck, which was already a mess of sleeping bags, movers' quilts, water canteens, baseball bats, tire irons. "Where to, sweetheart?" Larry rammed the key into the ignition.

"What makes for a good garden site?"

"A weekend hideout of a rich bastard who owns too many hideouts to visit any of them regularly."

The upside of being included on Ham's A list was knowing people with more than one house in more than one country. *"No problema,"* I echoed Larry, and suggested we check out Beth Hendon's once-or-twice-a-summer shack in Lafayette. It was a joke, but I talked up the property's remoteness from roads and from other houses, its treed grounds, its skinny, twisty, unpaved driveway. Easy to defend in postapocalypse days, I tempted. Larry grilled me on details: the layout of the shack, the physical contour of the grounds, estimate of total acreage. I told him what I remembered from the one time I had dropped off her out-of-town hunk of the moment, and invented what I didn't. "Sounds doable, pardner!" He shot out of the illegal parking space, and speed-merged into traffic. Behind us on busy Cole, I heard drivers hit their brakes.

The month was January. When Larry and I started our dig on a rise with a floaty night view, the cabin's windows were shuttered closed, the pool covered with tarp. Beth was smoking dope on the deck of Ham's houseboat and giggling her grief at the stars. She didn't spend winter nights in the cabin. The chance of her showing up in Lafayette was one in a million.

I didn't recognize the car throttling up the loopy driveway because it wasn't Beth's white Camry. I'd had to re–parallel park that Camry too many times or had had to drive her home. The car inching up the driveway was a dark green VW bug. It stalled halfway up the loop, and Beth Hendon tumbled out of the driver's side and lifted its snub hood. Beth was wearing the same short, dark sheath she'd grieved in. She wasn't a *thing*, but I worried about Larry. You popped up at the wrong time in the wrong spot on Larry's horizon, you became one fast.

Beth minced her way from the hood to the passenger side, reached in and helped a woman out. It was the Hairless Salome of the Wüsthof knives and Crate & Barrel platter. In the bug's cockeyed headlight, I saw Beth hold up and prop her against the car. There was a connection—moral, or at least poetic—between Beth, Salome, dead Fred, Larry, me, Ham—but I couldn't stay with it long enough to figure it out. I didn't have the time.

Mayhem in real time happens faster than in the movies. One moment I was standing on the rise near where Larry was drilling deep holes, feeling good about all that women bonding with women below; the next I was on the ground, cheek pressed into dug-up clumps of grass and earth, throwing up. One moment there was an efficiently lifted, ex-model's gaunt face; next a pulpy mess, exploding in record tropical heat like overripe fruit.

I heard the shot that killed Beth, but I didn't see the dying.

Larry was fulfilling the promise he'd made me earlier that evening: an alfresco date with mega mayhem. The vet who made it home from the ruby-red paddy fields is a survivor on permanent metabolic overdrive. The moralist's low-tech radar tracks the Larrys' guilt but not their pain.

I was throwing up in the starved light of a stooped moon because I'd nixed Larry's original plans for a beer and a blowjob; you nudge one block out of line, and all the neighboring blocks teeter and realign. You flee in the face of middle-aged lust in Sausalito, and before the night's over you end up in Lafayette, accessory to murder.

There's no accurate predicting, though, of the intensity and range. I had no idea what loco pleasure Larry would indulge in next. He did a brief celebration jig like he'd just made a touchdown with network cameras rolling, and yelled, "Shabazz! Shabazz! Shabazz! . . ."

I rolled over and lay on my back. The moon was a pale scar in the sky's star-pocked face. The dewy air was doused with vomit and sweat. I closed my eyes tight, and saw familiar veins like snakes squirm across my eyelids; I smelled charred scrub and singed flesh. When I opened my eyes again, Larry was racing down the rise to where the two corpses lay; he was plucking trophies. He hacked a thumb and a toe off Beth, who didn't have a head left to ravage, then he straightened her legs into a long, lean un-crossed **A**, and crouched with his head in its apex.

That's when I shot him. That's why I shot him. The why and when of that moment are joined like Siamese twins.

Each of us has two brains, one in the gut and one in the skull. It's true; I heard it on CNN. My skull-brain must have asked the why the very moment that my gut-brain was shouting the when.

All wisdom is visceral. I know to leave my dead to be discovered by somebody or some*thing* else.

I drove Larry's truck back to the Haight, and parked it in front of the same fire hydrant Larry had. There were no legal spaces left. With Larry's keys, I let myself into his apartment and helped myself to a few knives and automatic handguns, most of the lock-picking tools, a few of the bugging devices, and all the pills, powders and vials. No breaking and entering. No slipshod signs of petty pilferage. That felt good, but not great enough to make me careless. I slipped Larry's keys back in the pocket of his windbreaker still hanging from a lopsided peg, and left the bureaucratic business of discovering and reporting Larry's sudden absence to the landlord and the meter maid.

The three bodies on Beth's property in Lafayette were discovered by two kids joyriding on crystal meth, but it took them awhile to think of looking for a pay phone and dialing for help. The police chose to be tight-lipped about Larry's "gardening" equipment, leaving it to barroom detectives to deduce and to local journalists to speculate. Ham identified the bodies of Beth and the woman with the shaved head. He and Jess made the funeral arrangements. I grieved with them in public. In private, I celebrated. The dead women were the same age as Jess. Two stand-ins for Mother down. I was closing in.

Courtesy of a madman, I felt closer than I had to my bio-parents, but Ham, the Mr. Berkeley, aged.

Part Three

The lumpy, quilted envelope addressed to Jess arrived at the agency office eleven days after the death of Beth and Hairless Salome. I cope with the incident in Lafayette because I am careful about how I describe what happened. *They died.* Not *They were killed.* Not *Larry picked them off the way he must have Cong peasants.*

The envelope was delivered by Troy Tran, our stud mailman who sometimes took me karaokeing at the Mint.

"One cent postage due on this baby," Troy announced. "Don't you love it that the post office makes the sender pay these days?"

He has a radio announcer's voice. With his looks and his shoulders, he should be a TV anchorman, but he's taking acting lessons. It's the Flash's fault. The Flash is legend.

"So how come this package got through?"

"Come on, we're talking one lousy penny. And no sender's address."

"You want to collect the lousy penny, Troy?"

"How about a glass of Gatorade instead?"

I was the only one in that morning. Jess was chauffeuring an astronomer with a surprise hit book on his hands, *I Winked, the Stars Wobbled.* Otherwise it was a slow week even for late January, which I know from Jess is recoup time after the seasonal frenzy of coffee-table books, cook-books, how-to books for Christmas and Hanukkah gift giving. I had to field a couple of calls before I could get Troy a cup of iced water.

"The Unabomber's locked up, but I still wouldn't be in a hurry to open this one." Troy handed me the heavy package. "The grease stains don't do much for my confidence."

At least no wires stuck out. I checked the postmark. Oakland.

"But no return address," the mailman reminded.

"If you hear a loud bang on your way out, call 911."

"Well, have a great one."

My karma conspired with coincidence. I see that now. If my author-for-the-day, a woman named Rosie Rune who wrote feminist fables for children, hadn't been stuck in Chicago with a serious case of food poisoning, some other temp would have been in the office that afternoon. If Troy hadn't joked about letter bombs, I'd probably have weighed Jess's privacy against my curiosity, and dropped the envelope on Jess's desk for her to open. But that day my skull-brain didn't speculate on destiny and chance. My gut-brain dictated I grip the pull tab. My teeth did the gripping, and the ripping open. My face wasn't blown off by any bomb.

The sender was a joker. Packed in the envelope that I wasn't meant to open was a thin, poorly xeroxed stack of court transcripts about a murder trial, a couple of sheets of lined notepaper with diary-style entries handwritten in black ink, two syringes—the old-fashioned glass kind that

Flash used to shoot up the enemy with deadly serums—
tiny wooden matches in a box that had a picture of an
elephant-headed man with a Buddha-like paunch, and a
Post-It with the greeting: *You are the fox, my love for you
the bloodhound.*

A poetry teacher like Mr. Bullock or a sicko loco like . . .
Larry died, okay? I didn't kill him . . . well, Mr. Bullock
might have sensed connections; I didn't. Which was why I
scanned the transcript pages at random; which was how I
discovered a part of Berkeley Ham had kept hidden.

> PUBLIC PROSECUTOR: You admit that you are an unmar-
> ried woman?
> APPROVER: Fuck your institutions, man! I pick who and
> when I want to ball.
> PUBLIC PROSECUTOR: In addition, you admit, do you not,
> that you are an unmarried woman who is, however, not a
> virgin?
> APPROVER: I'm a free spirit. I don't have your bourgeois
> hangups.
> PUBLIC PROSECUTOR: Uh-huh! So you confess that you
> have carnal acquaintanceship of many men?
> APPROVER: What kind of trip are you on, man?
> JUDGE: You will answer to the point, please.
> BARRISTER FOR DEFENDANT: I take the witness's answer to
> mean that she is soliciting my esteemed colleague, the PP?
> APPROVER: Dream on, buster!
> PUBLIC PROSECUTOR: Did you have intercourse with the
> deceased male?
> BARRISTER FOR DEFENDANT: Please to specify per name
> and descriptive physical identification which deceased
> male since the witness has had many carnal satisfactions
> with many males.
> PUBLIC PROSECUTOR: Did you have intercourse with one
> Marcel Fallon, deceased tourist from Brussels?

APPROVER: I shared a cot with a Marcel Fallon in a Delhi youth hostel. I didn't sleep with him.

PUBLIC PROSECUTOR: Have you had intercourse with many males?

APPROVER: Many guys at one time? As in a love-in? Or do you mean orgies, porno films . . . ?

JUDGE: It is a well-known fact that youths in America consume large quantities of drugs and alcohol, and engage in pre-marital sex. The point that the PP wishes to establish needs no further corroboration for establishment.

PUBLIC PROSECUTOR: Thank you, Your Honour.

BARRISTER FOR DEFENDANT: But an unwitting corollary to that same point, Your Honour, is that my client, Sri Romeo Hawk, is only partially Western in origin. The more significant part of Sri Hawk is immersed in Eastern philosophy and ancient wisdoms. The PP is confirming what I have been arguing all along. The Accomplice-turned-Approver perpetrated sexual enjoyment on my client in order to coerce him into participating in her plot.

PUBLIC PROSECUTOR: Your Honour, the evidence will show that Mr. Hawk, having in-born knowledge of the sexual appetites and proclivities of Western men and women, exploited that knowledge in order to despatch her to the late Monsieur Fallon's room.

BARRISTER FOR DEFENDANT: I submit that my client, Sri Hawk, did not coerce this witness to perform sexual high-jinks on the deceased Belgian. In addition, I submit that the original transliteration of my client's surname was H-a-q, which Your Honour will confirm is a familiar Muslim nomenclature. H-a-w-k was the invention of Catholic nuns in Saigon. My client's mother, an illiterate Eurasian lady of the night with expensive addictions—"

PUBLIC PROSECUTOR: Objection! She was no lady, she was a prostitute. Also, in the absence of birth certificates of mother and son, questions of race, ethnicity, et cetera, are lacking evidentiary confirmation.

JUDGE: Objection overruled. Clarification noted, however.

BARRISTER FOR DEFENDANT: Mr. Hawk's mother took the infant Mr. Hawk to the orphanage with a cock and bull story about having found him under the bar counter. Therefore, I submit, Your Honour, that the East has played a greater part than the West in the life and character formation of Romeo Hawk. The witness was the temptress. She lured her victim, this Fallon fellow, into her hostel room and provided him with fatal enjoyment.

PUBLIC PROSECUTOR: But the witness visited the victim in the *victim's* room. The victim did not enter, I repeat the victim did not enter, the witness's room. The wretched truth is, Your Honour, the witness was a hippie from foreign, and not having sufficient funds to pay for food and lodging, she resorted to underhand—please amend that to *underbody*—methods of bill payment.

BARRISTER FOR DEFENDANT: Is that not further proof, Your Honour, of the witness's promiscuity? She cannot pay for roof over her head, so she sells sexual favors and pleasures for fiduciary gain.

PUBLIC PROSECUTOR: Objection! Sexual exuberance is an illness, not a commodity for barter. My client suffers from the disease of sexual exuberance.

BARRISTER FOR DEFENDANT: If that is an ailment, I thank God that it is an ailment that has not spread its contagion to this subcontinent. I shall not waste more of the court's time on the West's moral cancers. The rest of that night's scenario can be reconstructed by any simpleton. Like most Western youths, the witness is a frequent, if not habitual, consumer of contraband drugs. She was found to be in personal possession of sundry drugs for artificially inducing states of euphoria, aphrodisia and melancholia. I submit that she, the Witness-turned-Approver, slipped a large dosage of sleep-inducive medication, namely Mandrax, into the victim's alcoholic beverage. Then she executed her carnal designs on the victim's person. And when the drugged victim was rendered sufficiently drowsy by Mandrax, she garroted him.

PUBLIC PROSECUTOR: But how could such a slip of a young lady garrot an adult male with the athletic physique of this Mister Fallon?

BARRISTER FOR DEFENDANT: With her hair ribbon, no less.

PUBLIC PROSECUTOR: Objection! The marks on the victim's neck were made by human digits. They were not made by satin strings with which pretty ladies bind their tresses. We draw attention to the autopsy report completed on the deceased tourist from Belgium. The autopsy report indicates that severe pressure was applied to victim's neck and throat by means of exceptionally strong human fingers.

My mother'd committed follies on the other side of the moon, and now a lover or blackmailer was hounding her. It could be any flower child's story. Ma Jess had seen herself as a missionary; she'd made self-improvement her mission. Ben Franklin, turn over in your grave. She was the perfect daughter of her times: morality an "opinion call," idealism a means to an end.

All of it made crazy sense to them. None of it made sense to me. Their Asia was excess. My Asia was oppositions in perfect balance.

I felt inspired by Jess. *It doesn't have to be adversarial, Mother. You cracked under pressure; I won't. That's where we're different.*

I prowled the office, reaching into backs of drawers I rarely opened. The transcripts didn't have to be my only heirlooms. You never know: that's the American way. Discovery, it wouldn't matter how trivial, would enhance my self-inventions. Look and you might find. Anyway, what did I have to lose?

In the bottom drawer of one of the two filing cabinets that had INACTIVE/STORAGE labels on them, I came across an accordion letter file. In the *C* compartment of that letter file, bound together with twine and topped with a note in Ham's handwriting, *Tricia and I tied the knot in Vegas last night. Thought you might want these back, Love As Always,* were postcards Jess'd mailed Ham from places with pretty names. Surakarta, Seremban, Chiang Mai, Mandalay, Tabrīz, Ranpur.

My sweetest, dearest friend, If you could see my aura now, you'd understand why I had to leave . . .

and

This place is magic and I'm seeing in a new spectrum of colors, I'm feeling with a whole new velocity . . .

and

Today's lesson had to do with western attitudes to disease. R. is my lover and more, he is my guru, my teacher, my prince. He's taught me that illness is punishment for a past life's sins. Malaria, cholera, leprosy: they're our just deserts . . .

and

At R.'s command, I'm giving out herbal pills and potions to tourists so that their bodies and souls may be purified without their knowing it . . .

Stuck in the back of Ham's folder was a photograph of Jess in a peacock-feather tutu and of Ham in a penis sheath and nothing else. In the background, dancing around an oak, were other wood sprites in gourd-straps and forest nymphs in bird-feathers. I recognized the woman who had shaved her head for Ham. She had a thick, frizzy halo of red-gold hair. The hair could pass for a wig. Hats looked better on her. I slipped the photo in my pocketbook.

I should have been content just finding those postcards. It's wondrous, the self's capacity for growth and change. But Jess wanted me to find more. She hadn't destroyed any of it; she *wanted* someone—me—to come along. I scoured the files, dug into shoeboxes discarded on closet shelves, unlocked the petty-cash drawer, sprung the safe-deposit box Jess kept behind a sofa. And then I sat at Jess's workstation with the antique scribe's lap desk from India, trying to think like Jess, doodle like Jess, tap a nervous knuckle against the desk leg like Jess, and there it was, a secret compartment glided open in the antique desk. Inside that long, shallow space was a single snapshot. A mother and her just-born. Mothers look radiant, always; the just-born wriggly, helpless, uglier than garden slugs. My eyes were slits, hair long and black, plastered by heat, by afterbirth, to my forehead. It must have been *him* who took the picture.

Late that exhilarating afternoon, I dialed her number. "Jess, tell me what I can do."

"You've done enough," she snapped. "You show up and three friends are dead! 'Dying! Dying in the night! / Won't somebody bring in the light / So I can see which way to go / Into the everlasting snow?' "

One of Emily's, I assumed. When I made the call, I hadn't been thinking Suicide Hot Line.

"You don't get it, Devi. I loved Fred."

"I'm coming over, Jess. Don't do anything stupid before I get there."

"Someone has me in his crosshairs," she said. Her voice was mean and guarded this time. "Call him off, Devi."

"I would if I could, Jess. I want to."

"I've still got friends, you know. I'll be staying at Ham's, Fred expected it could happen, he was in the business, he said one day he'd turn over the wrong rock . . . but Beth's and Sandy's murders, I can't get over . . ."

So that was the gloomy woman's name. Sandy. Death finally demystified her.

"It's the end of something. We never expected to die."

I waited for more. It wasn't jealousy. A tsunami of envy rushed me forward. Envy of whatever made possible Jess's eternity of makeovers.

"Ham and I've been friends a long time, you know," she finished. And when I still didn't absolve her, she added, "Over twenty years. We even brought up the *m* word."

I know about the abortion. You didn't want a daughter.

"Can you picture me in the burbs? Orinda?" She laughed.

I sensed her uneasiness. The laugh sputtered into a smoker's hacking cough.

"You've started smoking, Jess?"

"No. I've gone back."

I know about your leaps off the Bay Bridge, Jess. I said, "That won't bring Fred back."

"No." She must not have covered the mouthpiece as she turned her head away and coughed again. "But it'll drive the ghost away."

"Did you say ghost, Jess?" I couldn't see Jess barefoot and pregnant in a Marin kitchen, but I could picture Fred's ghost fluttering above our heads at his own wake.

"The sins of my youth have come back to haunt me big time," she said.

I know about the blackmailer, Jess. "You are the fox, my love for you the bloodhound." Fred knew, too; now Fred's dead.

"Devi, there actually is one favor you could do for me."

"I was serious when I said I wanted to help."

"Take over my authors for the rest of the week?" The boss begging her employee to work overtime, while she hits on the employee's lover, without overtime pay.

Why should I mind? We go back a long way, Jess and I, in the rejection business. I've bench-pressed disappointment. *"No problema,"* I assured her. "Just leave it to me."

I hung up on Jess, and rode the 43 Masonic to Clay Street. Then I strolled around the block that the Leave It to Me office was on. Five times I circled that block. Five times felt reasonable, downright biblical, because I was following Loco Larry and Beth Hendon, holding hands, laughing and walking just ahead of me. Whatever animosity there had been between them that night in

Lafayette, they'd made up. No misunderstanding that couldn't be straightened out, Beth. No *problema* that can't be solved, Larry. In that generous mood, I ceased my pacing.

The "nobody's in right now to take your call . . ." tape was rolling as I entered the agency office. Then a cheery male voice came on. "You can flee, but you can't hide, *ma chère*. See you in Sausalito. *À bientôt!*"

Loco Larry'd prepared me for just this. *Things* were out there, he'd warned, ordinary things, harmless everyday things, but they were going to get me. They were stalking and baiting me. I didn't have Larry's night-vision implants, but I was starting to sense them, smell them, feel their damp heavy breath on my skin.

The voice on the answering machine left me alone. I updated the itineraries of Jess's authors for the week—she had a Random House novelist, a retired politician with a Simon & Schuster memoir and a New Age nutritionist with a MindWorks Press best-seller—faxed off the changes to the publicists, gave up the idea of a decaf and avocado-and-sprouts sandwich at Middle Grounds for another walk around the block, heard a Chihuahua bark insults at me and disclosed a phantom handgun to scare it, watched a tree weep leaves, then locked the office door against more *things*.

Two more messages from Jess's tormentor were on the tape. "You put me through hell, but I forgive you." And "Don't call me, I'll call you. That's a promise, *ma chère*."

I was about to call Jess when I remembered that she was with Ham in Sausalito, probably bunked down and in a consoling mode. The second-last time I was on Ham's houseboat, I made a baked-goat-cheese salad, Ham uncorked a bottle of Merlot, and for dessert we invented pleasures that women in their fifties, even buff ones like Jess, might find uncomfortable. Those good times hadn't receded far enough. I put the phone back on its cradle and speed-read two hundred and thirty-one pages of the Random House novel. If I got it right, terrorists from outer space kidnap the first lady and plan to clone her in the millions. When I got home to Beulah Street, past Stoop Man and the others, outer space didn't feel all that far away.

That night the Somali family invited me for dinner. It was more feast than dinner, and they didn't exactly invite me, I just hung around the microwave with my Weight Watcher's cabbage rolls in the kitchen we shared, and made an inspired monologue on the multicultural riches of San Francisco while the youngest of the Somali women stewed goat meat in sneezy-hot spices, then asked me to reach for a heavy platter on the top shelf to serve the bread topped with stew. They ate with their fingers, out of that one dish. Family bonding over a communal platter at the kitchen table. Take heart, battered crusaders for family values!

I let Emad—that was the med student's name—and his family get a decent start on the food, then joined in, tearing off bits of the soft, lacy, crepe-flat bread. Dunk in stew and chew. It was an act of good-neighborliness.

The family observed its own strict version of table manners. The man talked; the women and children listened. Everybody scarfed, fingers darting from platter to jaw with the quick daintiness of lizards' tongues. I kept pace with Emad's mother, and only half listened to Emad pontificate on newsworthy national events. His take on the city, the country, the world, came from some alternative information bank. In his world, the aliens had already landed and their kids were going to college. America's whole energy, its entire national military and economic output, was directed like a laser against Somalia for the killing of American marines. The press attacks on pious medical practitioners and their adolescent female patients were the clearest evidence. Just by positioning himself at the head of the dinette table, Emad had metamorphosed from the shy, smiling immigrant who avoided me in the hallway into the spellbinding oracle of Western civilization's end.

I had my own quarrels about the way that love and wealth were distributed in my immediate orbit, but this Somalian was so way off base that I couldn't dismiss it as comic relief from my agony over what my mother might be doing with Ham in Ham's bathroom or bed.

"For those without faith," Emad pronounced, in English so I wouldn't feel left out, "the end is now." His children stared at my painted-on tattoos. The women smiled at me, and demonstrated elegant finger-licking methods to keep the yellow-brown gravy from dripping onto the table. Someone down the hall was playing Buzz Cocks, very loud. I tried to figure out who, because I didn't want to have to listen to Emad keep shouting, "For you Westerners, it is code blue!" He had no right to target me for his apocalyptic harangue. "Before we've finished our supper," Emad went on, "the orderlies of the Holy War will be wheeling the West's corpse out of ICU!" He turned to the children. "What is ICU? Please define for our American guest."

Quiz and catechism.

The older of the two kids spoke for the first time at the table. "ICU equals 'Intensive Care Unit.' It is a place where the infidel die. The faithful are saved so that they can do good."

Father knows best.

"The infidel will pay!" Emad pledged. "You know what the Immigration people did to my wife at Heathrow? They took her away. They dragged her off to a room and they strip-searched her. They shoved their filthy fingers into my wife, *my* wife . . ."

I glanced at the women. They kept their heads lowered. I tasted shame as well as goat meat in the stew.

"I'm sorry," I mumbled. I was. But I could have said, I envy you, I envy the clarity of your hate. That, too, would have been true. I might've been questioned rudely, but not strip-searched, at Heathrow.

My apology cut short Emad's demagoguery. "How you like the food?" he asked me. Norman Rockwell's ghost floated in through a closed, grimy window. An immigrant family in an American kitchen sharing its bounty with a guest who has less than they do. Thanksgiving on the

Lower Haight. "My wife," he beamed at the young woman whom I'd watched stirring and stewing, "she is a very good cook, yes?"

"I thought she was your sister," I countered.

"Wife number one," Emad bragged. The cook smiled at me from across the table.

I smiled back. "Three stars, I'm a *Guide Michelin* scout."

Emad should have left the introductions at that. But he was in a good mood, maybe even a patriotic mood. "Wife number two," he continued, pointing to the second-youngest woman. "She is the children's mother."

Two wives? A bigamist on Beulah? Maybe the guests on shock shows on TV were more in touch with American reality than Ham and Jess were. I was living a tabloid life.

Emad gestured at the women I'd assumed were his mother and aunt. "Number three and number four." He counted off four on the notches of his fingers. "My grandfather could afford three, my father only two. I work harder, I earn dollars, I'm a family man."

He seemed to be eyeing me. I excused myself, holding my greasy hand high.

We were all tourists from outer space, passing through Earth. I locked myself in my room, changed into the T-shirt I wore to bed, stuck one of Larry's handguns under my pillow and finished the Random House novel.

Before it burned down last week, on Ellis between Larkin and Hyde in the Tenderloin, there was a bar with a green and yellow neon sign that read SNOW WHITE, ALL GLASSES GUARANTEED STERILIZED. That's where I ended up with Pete Cuvo, the Random House author, the night he read at Borders in Union Square. We started out with a late dinner at Moose's, browsed awhile at City Lights Bookstore, where Cuvo thrillers were prominently displayed, stopped for brandy-laced coffees at Tosca's but didn't run into Ham and Jess as I'd both hoped for and dreaded, watched transvestites shimmy at Motherlode, out–Diana Rossed with my *Baby Love* at the Mint and then went on to Snow White because around 2:00 a.m. Pete remembered his ex-marine buddy, Chuck aka Stanko, who'd gone through a couple of mail-order marriages before finding happiness as a roving bouncer in the Tenderloin. Chuck's last-known job, Pete thought, had been at a Vietnamese bar with a Disney name.

A good media escort is one who thinks fast on her feet. I looked for possibles in the Yellow Pages. Clarabell. Donald. Mickey. Minnie. Mother Goose. Snow White and the Seven Dwarfs. We took my tired Corolla to a Snow White I found on Ellis, and bingo! there was Pete's former buddy from his marine days, exercising unnecessary roughness on a bounced patron. Face pinned to the sidewalk by Chuck's boot, the drunk made invisible snow angels. Pete and I stepped over flailing arms and legs.

"Don't kill him, Stanko. Where's the fun in killing a neighborhood fuckface?"

Chuck took his boot off the pulpy, bleeding face. "Holy shit! Crazee Cuvo? Mad Dog of Moravia Cuvo? You Saved My Ass Cuvo? Tell me you ain't a ghost!"

Pete responded with a banshee shriek and howl.

Chuck turned his attention on me next. "Who's the beaut?" He poked me in the arm as he asked the question, putting me through his version of a ghost-check. Strip-search, Tenderloin style, lingering hands, probing fingers. I karate chopped Chuck. Flash had eliminated a border guard with one chop in *The Sadist of San Diego*. Flash's chop had broken the sadist's neck. I hurt my palm on Stanko's chest.

Some nights destiny puts up detour signs. Such nights all you can hope is that when the road's been repaved, it'll take you where you have to go faster, smoother, safer. I resigned myself to a long night of macho anecdotes. Pete and Stanko would go head to head burning hooches, hunting water buffalo with M-16s, startling Charlie out of his cover and upping the pussycount, which was what they'd fought the war for. For me detours were times to meditate. On bitter Emad, on Loco Larry, on *things*. Soon, very soon, a grand act of propitiation would be called for. I drank hot water with lemon, and stayed wired for clues.

In place of clues, Larry appeared. I stuck my finger in Larry's chest; my finger went through. He slid into the cramped, empty space between my bar stool and Pete's, and asked me, *"Et tu?"* And when I told him that I had to, he said, "You was my buddy," then he rocked my elbow into Pete's, knocking Pete's glass off the counter to the floor. Jack Daniel's splashed my dress. The stain unfurled like a flag as I squirmed off my stool. "Beat it, Larry!" I screamed. But he stalked me into the ladies' room, he forced me down into a crouch—Charlie as POW in an interrogation room—placed my chin on the clammy rim of the toilet bowl, stuck a finger deep, deeper, still deeper, into my throat and kept his finger there until I retched blood, guilt and shame all over the floor.

According to Jess's agency rules, a ME doesn't run out on her author. The night at Snow White, I broke Jess's rule. I left the bar by a back exit. I didn't bother with the courtesies of "Goodnight" and "Would you like a ride back to the hotel?" I didn't give a damn that my author was falling-down drunk and mugging-prone by that time. *"No problema,"* Larry counseled, "you got plenty *problema* of your own." He stalked me safely to my apartment door.

"Look, let's be honest, Devi," Jess said on the phone to me at the agency office. "It isn't working out."

"I'll have to call you back, I'm on the line with Santa Monica about the Slater tour. Are you at home?"

"No. Devi, put Santa Monica on hold. This is urgent. It's eating me up. I can't handle what you must think of me. I hate not being straight with people. We didn't plan it this way. Neither of us did. I don't know how seriously involved you were with Ham. I mean, we need desperately to talk about the situation."

"Are you at Ham's?"

"It just happened, there's no explaining it or apologizing for it. I mean, I'm not asking you to leave or anything. It just seems so awkward . . ."

"I'll have to call you back, Jess, the Slater development sounds messy."

"You're not listening, Devi."

"You feel guilty, deal with it. Ciao!"

The cyber-politician, Cindah Slater, didn't get to promote her memoir, *I Keep Going Home*, in San Francisco. She was too unpopular as a spokesperson to ever be elected to any one post, in any one city. She'd found her niche by moving beyond any issue. "It's not drugs, it's dealing with the effects of drugs," she'd say. Or "We live in a postrace society," or "I don't give a rat's ass about Medicare and balanced budgets. I'm looking to the real balance in this country . . ." She was accustomed to cheers, and when the cheers weren't loud enough for her as-told-to memoir in New York, Boston, Philadelphia, Minneapolis, Iowa City . . . she had her breakdown; she slashed her wrist in a hotel bathtub. The media stayed with the breakdown-and-suicide-attempt story. A television "newsmagazine" interviewed the limo driver who had chauffeured her the evening of the Breakdown. The limo driver was a middle-aged man, with a middleweight fighter's broken face and a spreading belly tucked into dark suit pants. He said, "You hire a limo, you get a bar, you get a TV, a cell phone, a fax machine, but no tissues to weep into. When you arrive at the limo stage, tears is verboten. So, I offered the lady my handkerchief. A personal gesture. She needed it, too, I can tell you."

I later saw the limo driver on *Ricki Lake* and *Jenny Jones*. He wore Armani suits on both. He talked of his childhood in Romania. "You need to have spent time in hell," he informed the studio audience, "to really appreciate heaven."

Pragmatic advice for all readers of the imaginary syndicated column "Dear Devi." Use your ingenuity, hustle being at the right place at the right time to turn your two-bit anonymous life into cash-cow celebrity.

FOR GUILT-STRICKEN IN SAUSALITO: Please expect a personal response to your request.

The West Coast publicity office of Cindah Slater's publisher'd been on the line, its fifth call, when Jess was angling for absolution. On the sixth call, the publicity people decided to cancel the rest of the Slater book tour because they couldn't make the suicide-attempt story work to sell $24.95 hardcovers. I spent half an office day canceling the memoirist's Bay Area appointments. "Due to unforeseen developments . . .": that was the line with the media, and with managers of bookstores.

The rest of my work that week was routine. I took messages, updated itineraries, tidied up Jess's files and alphabetized clients' books, starting with Ariana Ash, *This Age of Decadence*, and finishing with Herman Yanofsky, *I Winked, the Stars Wobbled*. I tried reading Ash's novel, set in Manhattan. East Side, not Nicole's or Angie's West Village Manhattan. The back cover described Ash as "the Edith Wharton for the nineties," but the thirty pages I scanned read like Martha Stewart hints on the care and feeding of East Side male availables. I tucked Ash back in her new niche on the top shelf, and pulled Yanofsky out of his cramped slot on the bottom. You didn't have to know zilch about astronomy to fall for this astronomer. Yanofsky was into the tragedy of heroic, dying stars, the comedy of parasitical planets, the wackiness of comets, the adolescence of the solar system. He played hide-and-seek with a billion galaxies I had known nothing about in high school. He walked on "dark matter" swirling between galaxies, and I followed. The universe was a cosmic aspic embedded with worlds instead of Mama's fruit salad.

Jess's tormentor called twice before I got to the end of Yanofsky's chapter "The Manifest and the Un-Manifest." The tormentor wasn't put off when I told him that Jess wasn't in the office. "The message is her friend called, called again, that is. Tell her, please, that the call was local, which is to say that the friend is in the vicinity." The voice was, strange to say, Frankie-like; I began to panic that it was meant for me. I mean, a filtered accent, something hugely foreign squeezed through the grate of English. The second time, I didn't give the blackmailer a chance to speak. He started with a Peter Lorre laugh when he heard my "Hello, Leave It to Me." I hung up before he'd brought that laugh to a sinister finish.

The MindWorks publicist, Mikki, faxed from New York to remind me that Ma Varuna would be traveling with her pet monkey and might need the services of a veterinarian, and then a second time notifying me of a change in M.V.'s flight schedule. Ma Varuna, formerly Bette Ann Krutch of Rehoboth Beach, Delaware, and her simian companion were originally scheduled to arrive on a morning flight from Portland. The second fax, addressed to me, not Jess, was handwritten on a sheet that had the elaborate Mind-Works Press logo—the serene face of Buddha with two Buddha-profiles sticking out of it in place of ears—but the fax ID at the top read *Fax Central* instead of *MindWorks*. *Due to the generosity of her nature, MV has given of her aura unstintingly to her legion psycho-nutrient-deprived admirers. In order to restore the healthfulness of a senior citizens' group in Multnomah County, she has decided to conduct an unscheduled lecture and levitation demon-*

stration in the morning, and arrive in time for her first print interview in the Bay Area. I got the publicist's message. Her author was exhausted, and wanted to sleep in. Portland was the eleventh city in her twelve-city promo tour. Get M.V. in and out of San Francisco before she has her collapse.

I faxed Mikki back. *Our agency delivers what it promises. Leave it to us, and relax.* I added a smiley face. Jess always personalized her faxes with smiley faces and exclamation points.

Then I looked up the names and phone numbers of three vets who specialized in exotic pets, wondered if, but didn't verify that, Purina sold monkey chow and finally locked up at the office and headed home to Beulah Street, speculating all the way back on how I could get my own celebrity-making sound bite by snitching on Emad the closet terrorist. But to whom? To the FBI? The INS? The IRS? I wished I could share my insight on Emad with Larry . . . I missed Larry. I'd had no clue I'd miss him so much.

Questions I never wanted answered: Was Ma Varuna a person or a high concept? Does the supply of mystics create the demand for metaphysical healthfulness? Did Bette Ann Krutch of Delaware find true happiness when she changed her name to Ma Varuna (translated in the kit as "Mother Wind-Goddess")? Do wind-goddesses give birth to typhoons, tornadoes and hurricanes?

I sat with a frozen yogurt and a sack of bananas in an uncrowded gate at SFO and went over the promo kit Mikki had couriered. *Vitality!*—Ma Varuna's third hardcover—was a tough read for nonbelievers. Not that I count myself among them. Still, I'm not a believer. The believer is a different animal from the gullible. The gullible grabs at quick fixes, turns how-to books like *Vitality!* into national best-sellers. I buy on impulse, but I mail in the warranty. Yield to hope, contain the betrayal.

I gave the book a chance. It had a pretty cover. Cheetahs lunged at lotuses in green-blue space that was either a forest or an ocean. I admired the art design, then the page that listed "Other Books by Ma Varuna," and after that the title page, and the acknowledgments page, but I didn't get past the two "poetic *pensées*" quoted as epigraphs. The word *pensée* was translated as "philosophical thought" in a footnote.

The first *pensée*, "Wisdom," was printed in italicized, gilt letters.

> *The sage stands silent on one leg*
> *on the snowcapped peak of Mount Everest;*
> *Master springs from bough to leafy bough*
> *Lassoing fruit and heaven with furry tail.*
> *The sage seeks but does not find,*
> *Master does not seek but tail-pulls in*
> *True wisdom, which is but emptiness.*

The second *pensée*'s title must have been a printer's error. "Nuclear Fusion" didn't make sense for the two-line riddle:

> *Mother's milk; cobra's venom.*
> *Equal delicacies when tasted in heaven.*

That one I got in the gut. Deadly today, lifesaving tomorrow. I called Ham's houseboat from the gate area on my cell phone. Jess's voice on his tape. "We are working on the new and improved edition of the *Kamasutra*. Please leave your name and number. We'll get back to you when we come down from heaven."

I returned to Ma Varuna's promotional material.

The kit included a detachable chart of a human body, divided and labeled like cuts of meat in a chart on a butcher's wall. In place of cuts like chuck, rib, rump, flank, shank, sirloin, the nutritionist's chart listed body sites for negative aptitudes, such as sloth, loutishness, mordancy, indecisiveness, narcissism, wrath. On the back of the chart was a recipe for "Ma's Bitter Melon and Fenu-greek Casserole."

The only publicity photo I found in the kit was that of a Mexican spider monkey. The monkey had a name: Master. The monkey's tiny eyes were glazed with an appealing desperate dreaminess. Were there on-line chat rooms for a wind-goddess's pets and spiritual daughters?

The monkey found me before I found the author. Master ignored the bananas, went for the chocolate-flavored frozen yogurt. One moment I was coddling a cone, my tongue was caressing sweet, creamy swirls; the next, my neck was lassoed by a skinny tail, and a spider monkey no bigger than a cat was licking yogurt-drip off the ridged sides of the cone.

"Low fat, I hope?"

I heard the Bacall-deep voice behind me, I breathed in the spicy sandalwood cologne, I succumbed—like Jess?—to the beauty and spell of a god or a devil. Among the slicker-clad passengers getting off the plane, Ma Varuna, in her gauzy silk tunic, her satin pants, her rich velvet cape and her silver-heeled T-strap dancing shoes, was more an apparition than a touring author in her attention-getting travel clothes.

Two factoids to pass on to Jess:

1. Deities don't glow
2. The devil's horns are retractable

Message to Mr. Bullock, may he burn in hell: You didn't have a clue about what made my poem a poem, but you started all this.

There may be some connection between energy level and levitation. Or Ma Varuna was on amphetamines. Her hands and feet led fidgety lives of their own. Her tongue raged, a flood-swollen stream, bearing me between mud-black banks on cruel waves.

"Your name, you say, is Devi?"

I sensed a trap.

"You know what your name means? Do you have the right to such a name?"

"As much as you have to yours."

"Mine was picked out of a directory of cult leaders and crooks." Ma Varuna laughed. "How about yours?"

"This is a free country." I kept my defensiveness flippant. "You can give yourself any name you want. There's a kid on my block who had his name changed officially last week. From Ralph Rinzoni to Anytime Anyhoo."

Not. Ralph Rinzoni was the name of the paramedic who mouth-to-mouthed the Stoop Man. I sat on the curb and watched the paramedics wheel him into the ambulance. The Stoop Man, spiritual guide to the Haight, was dead even as they carried him away. I knew he was dead, the paramedics knew he was dead, maybe the Stoop Man wired to intergalactical times and spaces knew his time had come, but he couldn't be declared dead until an emergency-room doctor scribbled *DOA*. I asked the paramedic who'd handed me the Stoop Man's Queen of Sheba tiara what his name was. "Mine?" He said he'd worked as a paramedic in three different states, he was good, efficient, didn't steal rings or watches, didn't go through pockets, had no license, just liked to be in on death and nobody had asked him that question. I needed to know. Grief would be easier for me to bear if I could say, Tom, Scott, Dan, Chris, whoever, lifted my neighborhood friend into the ambulance. "Ralph," the man said, "Ralph Rinzoni. No jokes about Rice-A-Roni, almost didn't come here because of it. You can call me Anytime Any . . . Do you feel okay? You don't look so good."

Ma Varuna was a holistic nutritionist, not a psychic. She couldn't divine my pain at the passing of the Stoop Man. "Ralph to Anytime is a matter of a legal change," she lectured. "Devi is not a name to find and choose. It has to find you."

I didn't have to believe her. Except that the Spider Veloce with the vanities *had* found me.

"Devi is the female gender of Deva," Ma Varuna went on.

"Thanks for the explanation," I said.

"But you are trailing no aura of light. For you Devi is a wrong name, the worst name. 'Deva' comes from the Sanskrit word 'shine.' You are not a shiny woman."

I hit the brake harder than I needed to at the next light. The monkey leaped off Ma Varuna's lap and hid in a pile of Fuji apples in the care basket in the backseat. "Master should be strapped into a child's car seat," I scolded.

"Master is my mother. Master is my father."

"It's a monkey."

"We see what we are capable of seeing. You see a monkey. I see a guide."

"Where's your monkey going to guide you? Back to a forest in Mexico?"

"Master's going to free me from the throes of bliss and pain."

For the remainder of the ride to her hotel, Ma Varuna concentrated on noisy breathing exercises.

Ma Varuna took in her first interviewer in gauzy black see-through tunic and harem pants and a brocaded scarlet vest. I hadn't expected nutrition alone to produce such abs and pecs. Jock Rice, the owner-editor of *Astro Sense*, an East Bay weekly, must not have either. From the way Jocko squared his shoulders inside his Eddie Bauer flannel shirt and puffed out his chest, anyone could tell that he was turned on. He squirmed in his chair. He couldn't make embarrassment work for him. He couldn't finesse his way out of anything coming to him, anything Ma V wanted to dish out. His Adam's apple bobbed and swelled. A sad little sinner with an Adam's apple is at a tragic disadvantage. Jocko, I sensed, was going down.

He fumbled in his backpack, but Master was on him, batting away his clumsy fingers and dragging the whole backpack to the center of the interview table and spilling its contents. Out came a tape recorder, cassettes, extra batteries, a pack of tissues, spearmint breath fresheners, herbal nasal spray, condoms packaged like a lollipop, a small papaya and a bottle of Odwalla's apple-ginseng juice.

Ma Varuna patted her lap, and the monkey sprinted towards her. She scooped the tiny monkey off the carpet, tossed it in the air, caught it and crushed its quivery face against her vest.

Jocko had some trouble with our watching him put his things back in the bag. I practice the Stoop Man Variation on the conventional wisdom that a woman should leave home wearing clean underwear in case she's destined later that day to be carried by a paramedic into an ambulance. Stoop Man chose his daily headgear with apocalypse in mind. Anonymity governs what goes into my pocketbook as I step out of the Beulah Street boardinghouse every morning.

Ma Varuna waited until Jocko had put away all items except the tape recorder. Then she sucker-punched him with advice. "Ejaculation is an unhealthy phenomenon. Such wastage of sperm is an offence to the Lord of Creation. The virile worship the *lingam*, but have no need of condom."

"Excuse me?"

The afternoon wasn't heading for a confrontation on Larry's loco scale, but I was beginning to enjoy myself. I owed it to the agency, though, to make sure the tape wasn't running.

"What's a nice Jewish woman of a certain age . . ."

Ma Varuna cut Jocko off by hurling Master at him. "Your question wants to know nothing. It wants only to reveal a bile-poisoned self. I do not answer narcissistic questions."

The monkey straddled Jocko's shoulder, leaned its face into the man's and twisted the wiry hair of his eyebrows into unsightly clumps. Of the many descriptions of Ma

Varuna that come to mind, "nice Jewish woman" was one of the more remote. If anything, she looked like some kind of ballet star, male or female I couldn't tell.

Ma Varuna clutched a handful of her tunic's hem, and arranged it like a veil over her head, then dragged it across her nose and lips in one silky, sinister movement. "The truth is that which the heart spits out over the tongue's barricade," she announced through the flimsy veil.

Jocko was planning to work through his virility hang-ups on my beat. As a temp, which I define as a worker freed of professional pride and of corporate loyalty, I wasn't about to let that happen on my ME beat. If the man had been tormented by kinkier sins, if, for instance, he'd been a seer of invisible malice, if he could detect auras the way Larry could or if he'd eavesdropped on in-audible threats from alien galaxies, I might not have called time-out with a patronizing query like "Room ser-vice, anyone?"

"I have the brew that Mr. Legume needs." Ma Varuna glided off the hotel sofa with the Flash's kick-boxing speed and strength. "Room service doesn't."

"Rice," I corrected. "Jock Rice."

"Get the kettle," Ma V barked. "Top shelf, hall closet. You'll find the cup and saucer in their traveling case right next to the kettle." She cheetah-walked across the suite and disappeared into the bathroom but didn't close the door. I asked myself what a woman from Delaware was doing reminding me of Frankie Fong.

The electric kettle wasn't the whistling aluminum kind Mama boiled water in for her midmorning instant Folger's. Ma V's was a sleek, foreign, ceramic appliance in its own vinyl traveling case, wedged between a carry-on and a satchel-sized pocketbook.

"Just get the kettle down," Ma called from inside the bathroom. The water was running in the sink. "I'll brew our friend my health special. You'll be a changed man, Mr. Jack."

I lifted the compact kettle and the cup-and-saucer set out of their cases and brought them into the bathroom. Ma V had a small Tupperware container of what looked like tea leaves open on the counter and the hot water faucet going full force. "Just leave the stuff there, I'll take care of it," she said. If I were making tea for myself I'd have started with cold water, but I filled the appliance just enough for a cup, unplugged the hairdryer and plugged it in. She pulled on a pair of disposable plastic gloves, the kind that you buy in pharmacies, not supermarkets, and measured four pinchfuls of the dried leaves into the cup. "I'll take care of it," she repeated.

I went back out into the sitting area where Jocko was sulking and Master climbing the drapes. "I guess I'll get some kind of story out of this," Jocko muttered. "What's she concocting? Something the FDA doesn't know about?" But when Ma Varuna emerged from the bathroom with the steamy cup, he changed his mood and mind. "What's in the brew, ma'am? A new Asian anti-oxidizing agent?" He'd already begun to line up great new body, effortless good times, romantic dates.

There's something to be said for the California epidemic of despair-deficit disorder.

"A bile eliminator." Ma Varuna, still wearing gloves, placed the cup and saucer on an end table close to Jocko. "Bottoms up!"

I liked the amber color of the infusion, but not the aroma. Master scrambled down the drapes and scooted into Jocko's lap. Monkey piss probably smelled as weird.

"Cheers!" Jocko upended the glass and downed the herbal broth in one breath-held-in draft, the way expendable cowboys do on TNT oldies just as the saloon doors swing open and the bowlegged Bad Guy struts in.

He went down faster, heavier, clumsier than any Hollywood extra or stunt person I've ever seen.

In reel time, dying cowboys hit the saloon floor, but in the twitchy, gory moment of going down, they don't crush to death cute spider monkeys. It's Master's accidental death that I still mourn. My sweetest dreams dissolve on Master's panicky screech.

"One down, and more to go." Ma Varuna punctured Jocko's forehead with the sharp heel of a silver sandal. Blood seeped and rimmed the edges of the small puncture wound.

"Why?" Reason, logic, the homey decencies of Schenectady: Were they delusions?

"I'm doing the fool a favor." She said that without a snicker. "Every soul needs a door."

"Why?"

"The body is a temporary home. The soul can't exit without a proper exit-hole."

If Ma V was right, if Devi is a name you can't earn or be given, if it's a branding iron that blisters cool, smooth flesh with a hot, metallic howl, I was branded "Devi" the moment that Ma V's slipper bored deep through a dead man's anemic skin and let out an unprepared soul.

The next few hours took Ma V and me places that didn't show up on the MindWorks Press itinerary. Maybe because Mikki, the MindWorks publicist, was destined to learn the Dee Law of Perturbation. In which case, Ma V's will cooperated with Mikki's destiny. Only the self-centered blame themselves for perturbation's damaging aftershocks. We survivors stay loose, we take small lateral steps out of the nasty reach of *things*, we dodge, we feint and, only when apocalypse opens up, do we deliver our knockout punch. The rigid, like Mikki, resist. Mikki now rests on a cot on the most secured floor of Creedmoor, doped into a serenity beyond misery and bliss.

Ma Varuna and Bette Ann Krutch: Of the two, which was the impostor?

I, a ragpicker of wisdom, hoard what I need. From Bette Ann's promotional material, I grabbed the Master Butcher chart of prime "cuts" of emotion. From Ma Varuna's psycho-nutrition, I stashed away hallucinogenic aphorisms. My favorite among her one-liners: "Destruction is creation's necessary prelude."

Zen masters have it too easy, answering disciples' questions with questions of their own. What I've learned—am still learning from unwitting teachers like Frankie, Al, Baby, Fred, Larry, Mother, Ham—is that for each question there are a zillion correct answers. *Mother's milk; cobra's venom.* Since both are right, and of equal value, pick the one that *feels good.*

A question for Bio-Mom: How did it feel when the Gray Nuns brought me to you in your Indian prison?

I was listing in my head all the correct answers to why Ma V aka Bette Ann K. should have "bile-eliminated" Jocko when she surprised me by taking off her clothes in front of me with the taunting efficiency of a professional stripper. Her first divestiture was her long hair. She flung the wig at my feet. The wig was of human hair, but I'd assumed the hair was her own. Black strands writhed like serpents around my ankles. Next, she shrugged off the vest. In the whirl of gold brocade and rich silk, I thought I glimpsed the twisted, accusatory face of Master. And after that, with gestures that were lithe, lewd but also mysterious, she freed herself of the long tunic of gauzy material. The torso she revealed paralyzed me with its . . . its oiled luminosity, its mean muscularity, its scornful splendor. I heard a flawed heart pound the arrhythmic beat of adoration. The harem pants shimmied to the floor. I heard Mr. Bullock's voice recite half a line. Not by then-you're-a-natural Debby DiMartino, but by Emily Dickinson. " 'You may have met Him . . . ,' " my junior high English teacher cautioned. The rest of the line was drowned out by Jess's ringing exultation. *"And wham! There was this . . . apparition."* Ruddy, roused male genitalia and silver heels mocked me. The apparition worshiped at its own altar with a frenzy of ecstasy or impudence. In that four-hundred-dollar hotel suite, the diffuse yellow light from a chandelier melted into the carnelian glow of sunset limning a tropical horizon.

Apparition, "narrow fellow," blackmailer: it spoke. "That silly woman, what's her name, Betty Lou? Betty Nan? Airport janitors will find her when they clean women's rest rooms. Meantime, Miss Media Escort! Do your escorting job and drive me to your boss's foxhole. I got a score to settle with that bitch."

"Are you planning to settle scores in the buff?" Ready whenever you are, Mr. Hawk.

Romeo Hawk costumed himself leisurely. Cream-colored silk shirt with French cuffs, vanilla double-breasted suit, pink silk jacquard tie, blue sapphire cuff links and tie pin. Snakeskin boots with narrow toes and stacked heels. A man who has spent time in Asian prisons values style. He was Valentino and Nureyev and Adonis.

He said, admiring himself in the hotel's flattering mirror, "You find me irresistible?" He had his back to me. "Every woman does."

"You're not my type," I snapped. I hoped I meant it.

"I don't have to be." He grinned. "I'm your father. I didn't come empty-handed, daughter."

He didn't contain his excitement; he didn't even try to. I braced for his gift—a burst of Saturday night special? —as he ran to the closet. He chucked the satchel-sized pocketbook and a flea market hatbox to the closet floor, then came to me holding out the carry-on I'd shifted on the shelf so I could ease down the traveling kettle. A green vinyl carry-on. The leather-panted Eurasian in the all-night diner where I hadn't paid for my Pepsi. No convergence is coincidental.

He read my mind. "The first time was accidental." He unzipped the carry-on. Cheap metal zippers need a lot of curses and tugs. "The rest perspiration." He dangled the carry-on just out of my reach. It looked light, hanging limp from his flat, wide hands. Karate-hardened hands. Flash hands. Killer hands. "The only gift you'll ever want, daughter."

I tore the carry-on out of those cruel hands and up-ended it on the rug. Five passports, that's all that fell out of the cheap vinyl bag. Five to be exact. Five passports issued to five separate names, but each carrying a photo of Jess's guileless face. I studied those thick, embossed and stamp-smudged official pages like a palmist reading life-routes and loveroutes.

Jess, too, was a ghost. She had inhabited five other bodies than the one I knew.

Bio-Mom'd paid her footloose way through hot, smoky Asia dealing in passports as well as dope. That, too, made sense.

The woman Fred Pointer had dug up as my biological mother and whom he had courted as Jess DuPree, successful Bay Area businesswoman, was also *Jeanne Jellineau*, b. 2/5/38, a citizen of France, the holder of a valid passport issued to her by the French embassy in Ankara. And she was *Sigrid Schlant*, a West German, b. 8/8/42, with a replacement passport issued her in Bangkok, where the original had been stolen. Also, *Veronica Alexandra Taylor*, born in Johannesburg, South Africa, on

6/7/44; *Magda Lukacs*, born on 3/9/43 in a German camp for displaced persons; and *Margaret Rose Smith*, a British citizen, born on 1/29/41 in Port of Spain, Trinidad.

"You want to take the first shot, daughter, it's yours. We're on the same side."

" 'Zero at the bone.' Dad?"

A vain man, he preened in front of the full-length mirror. "Whaa?"

"I'm on nobody's side."

Romeo slicked down a stray strand of his hair. He liked what he saw in the mirror. "Same as being on everybody's side." He shoved the mirrored closet door shut. "Don't elevate yourself to something you are not."

Like god or demon? Like a snake-thing? I took a swing at his face. He bounced back, grinning. "Dad forgives. Hello, daughter! Jolly good!"

Larry's old I ♥ MY ARSENAL sign was stolen off his apartment door soon after he vanished. I suspect Emad, but have no proof. The sign he painted especially for me I keep hanging above my futon. It reads: THE WORLD ACCORDING TO LIBERACE: TOO MUCH OF A GOOD THING IS SIMPLY WONDERFUL. Larry communes with me through the sign. The things you can see and touch aren't the *things* you should dread, he still mentors me. In that zombie hour of each night when I am not sure if I am dead or simply asleep, Larry and Liberace merge, sequined and giggling. Fear of the invisible is a good thing because it keeps you alive. Too much fear of ghosts is better, is simply wonderful, because it might also save your soul.

I didn't drive Romeo Hawk to Jess and Ham's floating love nest because of the 9mm he pointed at my head. I drove him because he was the scatterer of seeds from which I'd sprouted. Nature has no prodigality, no psychology, no sympathy. I drove him because he was *that place, the over there*, he was my poem of night, light and leaves. I was gambling on finding the maze's exit. Romeo did fancy twirls with the 9mm as we headed for the Golden Gate Bridge. He had the widest, surest hands I had ever seen.

He caught me staring at those hands, and said, "Don't get any funny ideas. These are my waste disposal units. They take care of expendable people. And the nosy."

"Like Jess's friend? Did they take care of Fred Pointer too?"

"Never inform, and never explain. That's the way I've always lived." He grinned. We could have been talking about a misdemeanor. "Jess's friend was. Now he isn't."

"Fred Pointer didn't start this," I fumed.

"There is no start, and there is no finish. Only process, you get the picture? I learned that from my trusted friend the warden, a Hindu."

"Fred shouldn't have had to die."

"It was his time, dear. And that bitch deserves serious attention from me. All those years in prison in India, how many deaths is that worth?"

"You're crazy!"

That's when Romeo raised the handgun to my neck level, and caressed my throat with it. Kept caressing the whole, slow length of the bridge.

Karma is groping your way out of a maze. You know there's an exit.

"You're not doing so badly yourself, little Devi. I always say genes will win out." Romeo was in a chatty mood.

Beg not for justice, and you won't end up straitjacketed in a padded cell or drowned in shallow water in Land's End. Make it happen!

Being stuck with an armed and crazy bio-parent in the rush-hour Marin-bound traffic organized my priorities. I didn't give a damn if I never found out details like the exact time of birth and name of birthplace. Go with the flow, as Fred Pointer'd counseled, keep your identity— your only asset—liquid. Breathe deep, relax.

"Take in the view," I said to distract Bio-Daddy. "We're proud of it." That "we" had slipped out, startling me.

"Nice Jag," Romeo agreed.

The Jaguar ahead of me had a bumper sticker that said IT'S NEVER TOO LATE TO HAVE A HAPPY CHILDHOOD.

"I myself prefer a Bentley," he went on. "Benzes are vulgar, Beamers prosaic."

"How about Alfa Romeos?" If it hadn't been for that Spider Veloce cutting me off that August day at the border, I'd probably not be chauffeuring my father to Marin this February evening.

"Too moody." He grinned. "Not worth the dough you have to shell out for it. Even as a kid keeping books for my father—hey, I forgot, *your* late grandfather; he owned a pedicab fleet—I could see myself in a white Bentley."

"White?"

"Snow white. Why? I'll tell you why." The handgun on his lap, he launched into the Hawk family history. "Because my father, Yves Haque, ran the Snow White Pedicab Company of Saigon. Our surname—your name—was spelled H-a-q-u-e by then. H-a-q to H-a-q-u-e was strictly an economic decision. A penniless man makes his way out of Peshawar or someplace equally filthy, and peddles cigarettes, chewing gum, dirty cards in *Indochine* cities. Ib Haq was an okay moniker for that man. His son upgrades Haq to Haque, buys himself a Eurasian whore for a wife, and makes what living he can driving pedicabs on the crowded streets of Saigon. Haque's son, yours truly, Americanizes his name to H-a-w-k, and procures for GIs to-die-for dreams. A procurer is not, repeat not, a pimp. We're talking imagination on the grand scale, Miss Dee. If you can supply satiety, there'll always be appetite. I could have been a millionaire. The war was good, very good, and damn your Berkeley peaceniks. The war was *great*, especially since Vietnam wasn't my real homeland. And then boom! my number one Bar-dolly decides to moonlight as the Cong's number one Tigerlady. You ever see American and South Vietnamese interrogators do their multicultural interrogation thing? Ever see a bargirl acupunctured with sharpened bamboo sticks? I got out fast."

"You turned her in?"

"Why not? A procurer's goal is profit. Patriotism and personal loyalty are strictly for the naive. Your boss knows that. She bought her way out of jail by turning 'approver' on me. That I could forgive. I'd have done the same in her place, but stupidity? She thought I'd rot to death in jail or, better still, get killed. The only peace of mind she's had for twenty years is thinking I'd never get out. Cads have more lives than cats."

"No one says 'cad' anymore." Frankie Fong said "cad," but he was imitating British actors in white silk scarves and paisley silk dressing gowns.

"Three life sentences still leaves me plenty." He pulled a letter or document out of the inner breast pocket of his stylish white jacket. The size and quality of the sheets of paper reminded me of the transcripts Fred had shown me when I was cocktail waitressing at poor Beth's club. I hadn't murdered Fred, but I'd killed him.

I kept my eyes on the Pollyanna Jag while Romeo Hawk read aloud portions from the court transcript. He said, " 'BARRISTER: You are claiming that the defendant bought five Kingfisher beers for the deceased female at Shakti Bar, which is known to be frequented by prostitutes and hippies. Five quart-sized bottles would be enough to fell a habitual alcoholic. Is your claim supported by personal and visual witnessing? APPROVER: I was there at the Shakti that night. I have twenty-twenty vision. BARRISTER: Can you deny that you also were heavily imbibing? APPROVER: That's irrelevant. He got her drunk so he could steal her passport and valuables, rape her, then garrote her. Garroting was a signature method with him. BARRISTER: You have this knowledge of theft, carnality and murder because you were present in the room and therefore you are not merely a witness to these deeds but also an accessory. APPROVER: Yes, I was present when he choked her to death. No, I wasn't an accessory. He cast a spell over me with that body, that smile . . . I saw him kill Astrid, I mean the deceased female, I saw him kill her and I did nothing.' What do you think, Devi? Is she guilty of accessorizing?"

Mother wore her guilt the way other women wore hats, scarves, earrings. The madman in my passenger seat didn't know how right he was.

I crossed the Golden Gate Bridge.

Jess must have thought it was Ham coming back with hummus and pita when Romeo and I clambered on board *Last Chance*. She popped out on deck through a narrow doorway, very smart in white jeans and white sweater, shouting, "Sweetheart, did they still have the whole wheat we like?"

I said, "Hello, Mom."

Jess shrieked.

"She is registering pleasure," Romeo explained.

Jess shrieked again.

Romeo turned on the charm, scooped her hand off the deck rail and kissed it.

"Long time no see?" I suggested.

With her free hand, Jess grabbed the deck rail. Scary biceps. She kicked Romeo hard once, twice, thrice, in the shins. Romeo's grin got wider and wider as each kick landed. *Envy my strength.*

Change that bumper sticker, Pollyanna. Some five-foot-nine, one-hundred-fourteen-pound children are miserable.

Romeo tired of Jess's kicks. His leg shot up and out and made contact with Jess's chest. He was faster than the Flash. Two more high kicks. Speed and malice total serious damage.

Jess moaned. "You can't have fucking broken out of that Indian jail. They kept you shackled. You're not here. You're fucking dead."

Romeo belly-laughed. "I'm not enjoying your nice company and the view of this nice bay," he said. "Bribery doesn't pay."

"Devi, call the cops!"

I backed away from Mom and Dad.

"That's what cell phones are for, Devi. Emergencies. Get 911!"

"We left in a hurry, Jess." No cell phone, no promo kit; only the care basket of waters, fruits and candies in the backseat of the Corolla.

Romeo snickered. "She doesn't like guns to her head." He shoved Jess roughly against the deck rails, bent her torso so far back over the top rail that I felt her pain in my spine.

"Let her go, please let her go."

Romeo nuzzled his chin in the mohair tautness between Jess's breasts. "Not bad for your age." Then he switched to his Ma Varuna–Lauren Bacall voice. "If roses are red, and violets are blue, our hate is eternal, and our love absolute. Happy Valentine's Day."

I'd forgotten it was Valentine's Day. Pappy would have left a box of Laura Lee by Mama's penny jar in the kitchen. Frankie would have sent his newest two dozen red roses. Or saucy stuff from Victoria's Secret. Probably both. To all his women. He'd have Fatboy Frontman take care of the Valentine problem. Nobody sent me flowers this year. Not even a Hallmark card. I'd have settled for one splinter-small ice-cold lead on whatever Romeo'd meant by absolute love. I hated Jess. She wasn't worthy of obsessive desire and claim-or-die pursuits. *He made me wanton*, Jess had lied to herself. She wasn't wanton, had never been and would never be, she was just another Central Valley hippie aging into Marin matron.

You didn't earn the right to pay Emily homage, Mother; I have.

"Get the hell out! Both of you!" Jess screamed. Then she sobbed.

"Fred didn't fall, Mom! He was pushed."

"Shut up!" Jess shouted. "Shut the fuck up! This isn't happening to me."

Something was happening to me. A little girl in a shapeless gray smock was being marched up the cracked cement steps of a small-town courthouse. Pariah puppies suckled on the saggy tits of a scarred, bony bitch in the courtyard. Movie lines merged with memories. *You shouldn't have. You was my mother.*

I rushed Romeo and Jess; I clawed, punched, jabbed, screamed and wept. Romeo eased his hold on Jess, but didn't let go.

"Why?" I begged. "They brought me to see you. The Gray Nuns. It was a long, nasty ride. The bus was packed. Why didn't you want me? I need to know. Why didn't you keep me? Why didn't you want to see me again?" It always came back to needs and wants. Frankie Fong had had that one figured.

Jess spat in my face. "I've never been pregnant," she hissed. "I wasn't that dumb. I may have been naive, but I wasn't dumb, never."

A flash, not a memory: *Judge, I'm not exactly dumb, you know. I've been on the Pill since I was fourteen, okay. That's not my kid. The dumb nuns got it wrong, but then what did you expect?* I must have been in the courtroom. I couldn't picture the place. I didn't see faces. Had it been hot or rainy that day?

Romeo pushed me away, and tightened his grasp on Jess's wrists. "Petunia, my pet, you can still rouse me."

Jess was flattered into a slight blush. I watched that grateful rosiness spread across her cheeks, and streak into the wrinkles around her lips.

Romeo took advantage of the blushing and softening. He whipped something metallic out of his pocket. Handcuffs. The man and woman who'd given me life were as strange to me as honeymooners from Mars.

Nothing is wrong with that picture of lovers on the deck of a houseboat in a neighborly marina. Of the men I have known, more have than haven't routinely carried handguns and sex toys, in addition to the usual wallet-stuffers like credit cards and driver's license.

"Petunia? Is that her real name?" Approver, Petunia: Jess had gone through more melodramatic incarnations than Debby DiMartino.

"My pretty Petunia. Alias Miss Free Love from Fresno alias Jeanne alias Magda alias . . ."

"What was your mother's name, Mom?"

"Get the fuck off my property. You're fucking trespassing. Ham? Why the hell isn't he back? How long does it take to pick up a pack of pitas, for chrissake?"

"What was her name?"

"Leave her out of this. Mother's been dead thirty years."

"Iris?"

"Get off the boat or I'll call the cops!"

"Not your boat, Mom. You don't have the right to order me off."

Romeo chortled. "You make me proud, little Devi. Now my turn to take over." He pinned Jess's body against the rail, unlocked the cuffs he'd only just put on her and closed his killer hands around her shoulders. "My pretty Petunia." He scrunched her shoulder blades together, and squeezed. I winced. She twisted her chin as far back over her shoulder as she could and spat. He laughed, let go of one shoulder, whipped out a handkerchief and wiped drool off her chin. "Keys," he said to me. "I need the keys to your motor, little Devi. You don't mind, do you?" He reached for my purse and yanked. The shoulder strap snapped. He stole the whole purse instead of just the keys. "I'll bring the motor back, not to worry, kid. Ta-ta!"

Dad shoved and dragged Mom; Mom cursed Dad all the way to my car. I couldn't have stopped them even if I'd wanted to. Dad had the 9mm, the cuffs, the strangler's hands. Maybe Mom's time had come.

I stayed on the deck, rocking back and forth on my heels in time to the rocking of *Last Chance*. The waves lapped the sides, higher, faster, stronger. I listened to seagulls, I sang with mermaids and waited for Ham to skid back into my life on the worn-smooth tires of his Triumph. And he did, could have been a half hour later, could have been longer than that; all I know is that by then sea and sky were communing.

"Hey, Day-Vee, hi!" He stuck his head out and waved. Women complications he could handle. "Your boss tell you she sent me for the one brand of pita bread they don't sell in Sausalito?" He hefted a small sack off the passenger seat and joined me on the deck. No ghosts, no purple auras, no angel halos: just a longhaired smiling man in a red polo shirt and white baggies, hugging dips and munchies. "What's up?"

What's up? Oh, nothing much, Ham. What's up? I'll tell you, starting with, Your friend and squeeze, Jess, Jeanne, Iris-Daughter or whoever, helped Romeo Hawk or Haque or Haq kill a total of seventeen men and women, nearly choke to death a no-name baby of no fixed address, bump off Fred . . . You want more?

"Jess just stepped out."

"In future, call before you show up." He led me into the cabin all the same. A quick kiss before emptying the deli items, then another kiss, this time long, rough and ardent. "Catfights prohibited on *Last Chance*," he whispered. He found my nipples with his teeth.

"I don't do jealous, Ham."

"That's why you turn me on, hon." The nibbling and biting continued. "So what brought you?"

"My author turned out to be Jess's best friend from way back when. He planned the surprise visit, I went along because he was the client. The surprise worked, I guess. They took my car and went for a spin."

"Which leaves us just enough indiscretion time, hon?"

I said, "What's that romantic aroma? The Ham Cohan Valentine Special Roast Chicken?"

"I lucked out. Happy Valentine!"

The secret of the sexes was suddenly apparent to me. Clueless jerks who can't get their underwear on straight still have the priceless women. It's on all the sitcoms, it's the imponderable, it's what makes the world go round. It's got to stop. I settled among beat-up cushions on the kilim-covered banquette and watched Ham rinse clean a wine-glass and paper-towel it dry before pouring a splash of Zinfandel into it. There wasn't more left in the bottle. He didn't reach for another wine from the rack behind him. He wasn't inviting me to stay for dinner.

The soundtrack of *The Big Easy* was playing on the CD player. "*. . . Got to be closer to you . . . wrapped in your arms, holding you tight, whispering faintly, baby, deep in the night . . .*" Ham and Jess had been getting in Valentine mood when we *apparitioned* on the houseboat. You kill the past only if you have the know-how to survive hauntings.

I leaned a lazy finger on the rewind button. When I let it up, the singer was reminiscing about lace curtains, willow trees, rustling bedsheets. I didn't have to listen to someone else's nostalgia. "*. . . the smell of the morning in the rainy lane . . .*"

A wartime memory that Larry once shared popped into my head. "You know what I remember best about the place," he said. "The swallows. Blue swallows, goddamn swarms of them getting in your face. It was beautiful! I wouldn't have missed Nam for anything."

I didn't care if too much Dexedrine had turned crows and sparrows into a blue blanket of swallows. Eighteen-year-old Larry Flagg had gone into the war with a fuck-with-me-and-you're-dead attitude; Loco Larry had come out of it with a postcard-pretty souvenir.

I turned up the volume. *"If I said that I loved you, would you turn away . . . well, that's all right, baby, 'cos I already know . . . believe me, baby, we got no choice . . ."* I saw Larry, Ham, me, chasing aquamarine birds down terraced fields of emerald. " 'Come here,' " I sang along with the tape, patting the cozy space beside me, " 'come here, come here, come here, got to be closer to you.' "

"Got to check on the roast," Ham said. "Wonder what's keeping them, must have a lot to catch up on." He slipped on a starched, white, professional-chef's apron. "The trick to perfect chicken is a five-hundred-degree oven. I learned that from my last ex."

I kicked my shoes off, and stretched my legs out on the banquette. The big toe of my right foot touched the boom-box's STOP button, then traced huge hearts on the plush velvet nap of a cushion. I felt like pulling up anchor, dancing naked on deck, steering *Last Chance* into the eye of Hurricane Faustine. The boat tuned in to my mood, rocked on violent waves.

Ham got off on the subject of ex-wives. "Tess gave me the apron," he said. "You've met Tess, right? She was at Fred's wake?" He yanked down the door of the oven. A whoosh of hot, spicy air made his face red. "The mitts, cap and apron were her divorce-anniversary present. She was a CIA dropout."

"You were married to a spy?"

"CIA as in the Culinary Institute of America." Ham was recharging bitterness. "I got the Wüsthof knives in the settlement, the Chinese meat cleaver, the Japanese woks, the All-Clad pots. She kept the house."

I arched my neck. Frankie once told me that I had the sexiest neck and clavicle he'd ever seen. Ham didn't notice the seductive stretch.

"There's justice, though. In the Oakland fire, the house went up in smoke."

"What do you have to be so bitter about, Ham?"

He caught me eyeing the table set for two, the speckled orchid, the colored candles. "I'm not bitter. Who says I'm bitter? Did I ask for any insurance money?"

"Thanks for inviting me to stay for dinner," I joked. "I'd love to. How about a splash more wine?"

Ham reached behind him and plucked the bottle nearest him off the wine rack. It was another red. "Who's this friend that Jess's dumped us for? What's he written?"

"She met him in Asia."

"Oh, Asia. She really did Asia." He uncorked the bottle. "That makes the guy a hippie burnout."

"If you're part ethnic Chinese, part French Vietnamese, definitely part Pakistani and part you-never-figured-out-what, what does that make you?"

"Not a bad Merlot," Ham said. He carried the bottle and two paper cups to the banquette, and slid in beside me. "The city council in the People's Republic of Berkeley?"

I unlaced his running shoes. He finally took the hint, and played along, easing his feet out of the shoes. I peeled off his socks. No Mona Lisas on these socks. Just over-washed, yellowing white absorbent cotton. "And if you add half Californian to it all?" My toes stroked the feet's pale, clammy arches.

Ham kissed me on the lips. "Trouble?" He kissed me again.

"Force of nature," I reminded him.

"A fault creep," he amended, working on the metal button of his baggies.

"What's that?" I shrugged my shirt off.

Ham explained between kisses. About creeping and gliding and sliding movements along fault lines, pleasant pressure—"think of yourself as the Bay Area with fault lines running through," he said, "and your body is being worked on by a master masseur"—and then, wham, bang, whoa! the Big One breaks the body in two. He calculated creep rates with his lips on my fingers, slip rates on my toes. "Happens every hundred years or so," he whispered. "I don't want to be around for the Big Quake."

A quickie on a banquette in a houseboat may be no competition for acid-high sex with god-demon-snakeman, but for one nanosecond that night my brain could sleep. The immediate past and the about-to-happen both re-ceded. It was my oldest past that suddenly surged forward.

I was on a country bus, tasting dust and diesel. My new Bata sandals were wedged between someone's dirty metal trunk and someone else's stacked-high baskets of live fowl. My feet were going to sleep inside the pretty canvas shoes. The man beside me said to pinch the littlest toe of each foot. The man next to him kept spitting out the open window. His spit was the color of blood. I imagined blood-red betel-juice stains on the sister's funny clothes.

I am crying because the woman is crying. I can hear long, low sobs again, smell vomit again, press my face deep into Mommy's lap again. Daddy shouts, Shut her up or I'll do it myself. Mommy giggles. I want for us both to get back in the car again. I want for us to drive home. I don't want to listen for the grass to absorb a body's clumsy fall. This is not the first time I've buried my head in Mommy's lap so I shan't have to see or hear or know. Callused hands grip my throat. The world wraps itself in blackness.

Better that I had been the fetus Jess aborted. "Ham," I murmured, "why didn't you ask Jess to marry you?"

"The times, love. Marriage and commitment were for the bourgeois." He tucked his shirt back into his pants.

"You should have married her." I kicked Ham's shoes and socks across the floor. The kick was harder than I'd intended. One shoe thudded against the base of the counter. A bowl of olives crashed to the floor. They were the big, green, deli kind, an almond jammed into each of them. I didn't make a move to clean up.

"But then we'd never have met." Ham ripped lengths of paper towel. The bowl was a fifties stoneware ugly, the kind that shows up in decor magazines. The chipped pieces and china flakes were easy to pick off wetted paper towel. The olives left a dull smear on the polished wood floor. He tossed the clunky, squishy garbage and raised his paper cup of wine. "To roads not taken!"

"You'd have spared me my . . . my violent propensities."

"Propensities?" He laughed. "I like your violent propensities. Sounds like a designer perfume. Pro-*pen*-sity by Devi Dee! Propensity. Give me a break!" He ambled over to where the other running shoe had scudded to rest. "Anyway, what's my old life with Jess got to do with you?"

"Everything."

He was on his hands and knees, fumbling for socks, when we both heard the footsteps out on the deck. One pair of shoes with hard leather soles that slapped wood. Ham scrambled to his feet. Not Jess's sandals, definitely not Jess's power-walker stride. I couldn't tell from his face if he was anxious or if he was relieved. "She couldn't have been in a car crash, Dr. Watson," he said. "That doesn't sound like cop feet bringing bad news."

Romeo cheetah-walked in on us. I don't know what fabric his vanilla suit was made of. No stain, no crease, undermined its elegance. Only his eyes had a jailbird glower. He said, those eyes on Ham standing awkwardly with socks in his hands, "We had our chat, little Devi. Very satisfactory."

"Ham Cohan." He balled up a sock, dropped it, held out a hand. "Hey, man, where's Jess?"

No match for Bio-Dad. Poor Ham, caught in one of fate's sting operations. I wouldn't let him end up expendable.

"In the car." Romeo thrust out a hand. A sapphire cuff link winked in lamplight.

"She shouldn't have trouble parking." Ham gave the killer hand a quick, polite shake. "There were lots of spaces when I came back from the store. Anyway, can I get you a drink?" He shuffled to the galley, stretched for a wineglass. A real one, not a plastic cup.

Romeo joined Ham, reached across the butcher-block counter of the galley and picked up the opened bottle.

I felt woozy at the coziness of it all. "What's Jess doing in the car?"

"None of this sissy sweet stuff," Romeo said. "I need a real drink."

"What's she doing?" I repeated.

"How about a beer?"

Romeo swiveled his torso a half dozen times. A workout freak warming up for action. "Practicing breathing, little Devi." He laughed.

"What?" Ham stuck his face in Romeo's. "Who the fuck are you?"

"Who do you want me to be, Mr. Movie Man?" Romeo batted Ham's face away with his palm. "And she isn't doing a very good job of the breathing thing, Movie Man."

Ham grabbed the Merlot bottle and cracked Romeo but not a good one. The vanilla suit showed up pink streaks and blotches.

Romeo clicked his tongue. "Not much good at rough stuff, are we, Mr. Movie Man?"

Ham lunged for Romeo's tie. Romeo was a man of quicker reflexes. He gripped Ham's throat in those killer hands. "Big-stick bullies, you Americans," he sneered.

Ham's eyes bulged, his knees sagged, his voice box let out gaspy, growly sounds. When Romeo finally let go, the body thudded to the floor. I jumped.

"What was that?" Romeo grinned. "A quake?" He hauled Ham's body by the feet inside the galley ell. "There was this warden I had a nice thing going with, hash for deutsche marks and pound sterling. The warden chap went down heavier than Mr. Movie Man, and he couldn't have weighed more than sixty, sixty-five kilos."

"What did Ham ever do to you?" I crawled as far from him as I dared. The cabin was cramped, but not with the kind of furniture you can crouch under.

"Nothing." He lifted Ham's limp body by Ham's gray ponytail nearly off the floor. "Everything." He slammed Ham's head, facedown, on the butcher-block counter, and pinned it with an elbow. "How much blood does a dead wimp bleed, little Devi?"

I threw up on the scatter rug, splattering Ham's running shoes.

Romeo laughed. "Don't spoil the fun." He snatched the Chinese meat cleaver off its galley wall peg. He whacked the blade on the base of Ham's neck. Whack! Whack! The blade got stuck in Ham. "Shit! I've lost the wrist, the snap. No practice." Romeo kept cursing as he worked to ease the blade out of bone.

I pressed my face into the rug; I smelled the sour smells of Ham's shoes, my vomit. I heard a final swish! and crack! Then the thump of Ham's severed head falling to the floor.

Romeo nudged me gently with his boot. Snakeskin rubbed my arm. When I squinted up, he was standing over me, cleaver in hand, and sucking on a miniature bottle of whiskey, the kind Pappy saved from plane trips. FREEZE TAPE.

"Need a drink?" He pulled another bottle out of his pinkish suit pocket. This time it was vodka. "Take a sip, go on." I thought of Aloysius Fong hitting the bottle in the wings, just before going onstage. Nerves, not guilt. "Hey, what was that?" He staggered.

I'd felt the wave too. "Never spent time on water?" I mocked.

"What do you keep in your waters? Jaws?" He stumbled again.

Violent propensities. The sea has them, the Earth rocks with them. I claim my inheritance, kneeing Bio-Dad so hard as he tilts his head back to draw from the tiny bottle that it tumbles him. TAPE ROLLING. The cleaver fuses to my arm. It soars and plunges, soars and plunges. "Monster!" I scream. I keep screaming as I cradle Ham's tormented face to my bosom. I am screaming as I dial 911.

Epilogue

Physicists and fantasists suspect that someday there will be one simple equation to express and explain all the problems of all the galaxies. My big toe, which got Ham all horny, is also the TOE: the Theory of Everything. The mysteries of our universe become more mysterious as they grow ever more accessible. The symmetry of asymmetry.

What was it that I'd read in Yanofsky's *I Winked, the Stars Wobbled*? *The world you see isn't the world you get. Ninety percent of it lurks out of your sight. Invisible matter is the cosmic glue holding reckless galaxies in place.*

I am that dark, ghost, *thing*.

The quarks and electrons that make up villains and heroes also make the coffins we're laid to rest in, and the earth we molder in, and the maggots we fatten, and the stars that shine on us after our worlds vanish.

Destiny works itself out in bizarre loops. I made the 911 call. Domestic dispute, I told the dispatcher. Let them find out how bloody. I heard the urgent police sirens, I waited a long while for the waist chains, handcuffs, leg shackles. And just when I prayed for my misery to be over, the waves rocked wild and heaved *Last Chance* free of its moorings. The houseboat skimmed a molten gold sea carrying its cargo of dead and living towards a horizon on flames, I heard mermaids sing and police sirens screech, but not for me, not that night the Big One hit, with fires rimming the Bay like some nighttime eruption, with the night sky pink, reflecting off the fog, the sparks flying down like fiery rain, sky hissing into sea.